Layla's Unwanted Husband

The Buckingham Sisters, Volume 2

Robyn C Rye

Published by robyncrye, 2023.

LAYLA'S UNWANTED HUSBAND

First edition. August 18, 2023.

Copyright © 2023 Robyn C Rye.

ISBN: 979-8224819553

Written by Robyn C Rye.

Also by Robyn C Rye

Farnsworth Sisters
Marrying a Rogue
Rescuing Hannah

The Buckingham Sisters
Lady Maggie's Challenge
Layla's Unwanted Husband

The Evans Family
Sometimes Love is not Enough
Still the One
Moving Forward

Standalone
One More Chance
Lady Jayne's Reputation
Third Time's the Charm
Can't Stop Loving You

The Marriage Scam
An Unlikely Match
Searching For You
The Unexpected Suitor
The Lady and the Duke
Starting Over
An Unforgettable Stranger
The Duke's Revenge
The Temporary Wife
Against The Odds
Betrayed
No Good Turn Goes Unpunished
Lady Eloise's Soldier
Lillian's Forbidden Beau
Remember Me
Always Second Best
When One Door Closes
Coming Home to You
Chasing Shadows
Fool Me Once
Deserting Lady Audrey
My Unlikely Saviour
Lies and Deception
A New Beginning
Julia's Second Chance
The Hidden Enemy
The Maiden's Redemption
Miss Elizabeth's Season

Copyright © 2023 by Robyn C Rye

Author's message

I am an Australian author, so the spelling of some words may differ from that of the American dialect.

Thank you for joining me in telling the story of Layla and Beckett. I hope you liked their story as much as I enjoyed recounting it.

If you enjoyed the book and have a moment to spare, I would appreciate a brief review on the page or site where you purchased the book. Reviews from readers like you make a massive difference in helping new readers find stories like *Layla's Unwanted Spouse*. Your help spreading the word is appreciated.

Thank you!

robyncrye.author@gmail.com

Chapter One

Even though Layla had the upcoming season to look forward to, she missed her sisters, Maggie and Esme, who had completed their first season with her. Both her companions from last season were married: Maggie rather quickly to save her reputation, and Esme was in a love match with Lord Ben Reinholt. Layla shook her head; the way the evil Duke had blindsided her still rankled. Worse still, Maggie had tried to tell her he was not a good man, but his status and wealth convinced her that he was the man for her. This season, she would not let her Mother's desire for an elevated position in society influence her or a man's status and title. She wanted a good man to treat and care for her well.

Layla looked around the shop at the array of fabrics. Her wardrobe needed an update, although she could only wear pastel colours as a debutant. Would anybody but her maid know if she reused last year's dresses? It was hard to get excited about new dresses when they looked the same as those in her wardrobe at home, but her Mother had insisted she update her gowns, so if she returned home empty-handed, she would be in a world of trouble. Tilly, her lady's maid, lifted a bolt of fabric.

"What about this one, Miss Layla?"

Layla looked at the cloth Tilly held aloft and nodded.

"I like that one because while it is pastel, it has a dark red thread running through it."

It took another hour for the girls to choose the material for the new gowns. Layla glanced out the window. Jack, the bodyguard who had tried to keep Maggie safe during her early marriage, stood under the awning in front of the shop. Layla tapped on the window, and Jack looked back and blew a shrill whistle. Wherever the carriage had moved to after offloading her and Tilly, the whistle would recall it. With both girls carrying packages, they exited the shop to stand under the awning next to Jack as they watched for the carriage's arrival.

"Miss Layla, if you hand me your packages, I will help Tilly into the carriage, and once she has placed the parcels on the seat, I can help you. Without the parcels, it will be quicker for you to enter the carriage, and you will stay drier."

Layla nodded her agreement, and Jack and Tilly hurried from under the awning to the carriage door. Once Tilly was inside, Jack motioned for Layla to approach the coach. Layla rushed towards the vehicle with her head down to stop the rain in her eyes. One minute, she was moving swiftly; the next, she was flying through the air. Layla landed on the pavement with a thump, and her momentum smashed her head against the walkway. Tilly let out a shriek, and she and Jack rushed to the inert figure of their mistress.

"Tilly, see if the modiste has smelling salts."

Jack rubbed Layla's hands while waiting for Tilly to return, trying to rouse her. A glance over his shoulder revealed a tall gentleman who was cursing roundly. Once Tilly waved the salts under Layla's nose, she awakened, and with assistance, she sat on the wet pavement, gathering her wits. The man who had bowled her over moved closer and said, "Damnation, woman, couldn't you look where you're going? I was late before this fiasco, and now I'm not only late but also wet."

Jack, Tilly and Layla gaped at the man.

Gathering her composure, Layla held her hand out for Jack to help her to stand. She hung onto him in an unladylike way until her head stopped spinning, and she could stand alone.

Looking down her nose at the gentleman, Layla said, "You are a ruffian dressed in a gentleman's attire. You were more to blame than I and haven't even enquired about my well-being. Rush on to your dratted meeting, but beware of other pedestrians who might not be as easy to push over as me."

The man met Layls's put down with another string of curses, some of which included the words high and mighty and pampered princess. Despite the rug Tilly wrapped around her mistress, Layla's body shook; the cold and the incident combined made her edgy. When they arrived home, Layla sent Tilly to change out of her wet clothes and asked Cummings, the butler, to have the footmen set up a bath for her. As Layla relaxed in the tub, she reflected on the incident on the pavement. The man's response was so furious that he took all of them by surprise. Never before had she encountered a man with so few manners and no concern for others. The pounding headache that thumped in her head pushed aside her recollections, and when Tilly helped her from the bath, Layla crawled into bed to nap before dinner.

It seemed only minutes later when Tilly woke her to dress for dinner. Layla's headache had subsided, although a slight pain lingered. As she sat for dinner, Lady Buckingham scrutinised Layla.

"Goodness, my dear, you spent half the day in bed and still look under the weather. What ails you?"

As Layla recounted the incident outside the modiste's shop, her Father frowned with concern.

"You say the blighter never introduced himself or enquired about your well-being?"

"No, I didn't hear the first curses, which Tilly said were vile and numerous, but once Jack helped me to stand, the curses were about a pampered princess and being high and mighty. I concede I may have been careless in rushing for the carriage, but he knocked me unconscious and tried to blame the entire incident on me."

Lady Buckingham tutted. "There is no accounting for the type of riff-raff walking the streets these days. What is the world coming to if a lady can't visit her modiste without being injured?"

"Should I accompany your Mother to the modiste's to see if she recognised the man? I'm unsure what I can do if we identify the blighter, but surely even a belated apology would be better than nothing."

"It's unlikely she recognised the man because he was a stranger, not someone likely to visit a modiste, although his suit looked well-made. I will be well again in a few days, and the incident will make me more cautious on the walkways in future."

Chapter Two

Layla was nervous about tonight's event. It was her first outing since the disaster, which marked the beginning of her first season. Would others shun her after all that went on last season? She had ended her engagement to Lord Windsor, so there could be no backlash from that, but after Maggie's kidnapping and the death of the evil cad, there was plenty for the ton to gossip about. She knew her Mother was also anxious about the night, so the silence in the carriage on the way to the venue was not unexpected.

Once Layla greeted their hostess for the night, Lady Buckingham weaved through the crowd, greeting people and encouraging gentlemen they knew to enter their names onto Layla's dance card. It seemed that people were willing to forgive last season's missteps, and for that, Layla was grateful. For the most part, the gentlemen chatted about inconsequential topics, although a few tried to encourage her to discuss the abduction of Maggie and the subsequent death of the Duke. Layla was firm about refusing to discuss the kidnapping because she knew the men enquiring wanted a previously undisclosed detail to wow the ton with. Gossip was currency in the ton, and Layla did not intend to fuel the gossip mill. She did, however, remember the men who sought gossip and vowed not to dance with those men again, although, as they had not come away with extra gossip, she doubted they would ask.

When supper time arrived, Layla and her Mother visited the retiring room and returned to the supper room once most people were seated. The tables were full, and Lady Buckingham asked an acquaintance if they could join her and her partner. Layla ate slowly; her Mother insisted that Layla dish a minuscule meal, and she tried to make it last until supper finished. Layla considered the practice of serving tiny meals to the ladies to be an absurd tradition. Unquestionably, the men here didn't believe healthy young women could survive on such small amounts of food. Layla shook her head and looked at the couple leaving the tables. Perhaps she would need to reevaluate her opinion of the men of the ton; she feared that most of them believed a woman could survive on a few lettuce leaves and a couple of carrots. She smirked; what a shock the husbands must get when their new bride loaded her plate at their first shared meal.

After supper, Layla's dance card was almost complete, but even though she smiled prettily and feigned interest in the boring conversation, not one of the men sparked her interest. Were the men last season as dull and staid as this, or had her imagination played tricks on her, making them seem more interesting than they were? Heaven forbid if Maggie and Esme were to marry the only two exciting bachelors. Lady Buckingham smiled at an acquaintance and said, "We are fortunate, Layla. Most of the guests seem willing to overlook last season's troubles. Have you danced with any men who caught your interest? Unfortunately, as this season is your second, you might have to aim lower than before we met the Duke."

"I have not danced with anyone interesting; however, this is the first event of the season, so I needn't get too overcome by my lack of enthusiasm for the men here. I have the time to find the right man, and after last year's mistakes, I will not let status or wealth sway me. I want a good man, and as long as he can support me, I will be happy."

Lady Buckingham huffed, and Layla knew that, despite last year's disaster, allowing the Duke to court her, her Mother would still look for a man with a title to marry Layla. For the time being, Layla let her Mother dream of titles, but when the time came, Layla would decide about the man she married. Esme and Maggie had made love matches, and while Layla doubted that was on the card for her, she wouldn't rule it out.

As they travelled home that night, Layla remembered how tedious the last season had been with the constant round of social events and the endless morning calls on people that her mother aimed to cultivate. Layla wondered why her Mother cared about the opinion of the snobby, aristocratic women who would cut you down as quick as a flash if they deemed you had done something wrong. The women never disbelieved a rumour, and with malicious delight, they spread the latest on dit, whether truthful or not.

Layla remembered how glad Maggie was when she and Theo left for the country shortly after their marriage. She had said that in the country, there was no need to associate with people you didn't like in the hope that they would invite you to social occasions. Did her sister have the right idea? Layla's confusion regarding her place in life was something she couldn't discuss with her mother; without Esme and Maggie close by, she had no friends with whom to discuss her concerns. Layla's preoccupation with society and the ton generally took a back seat after her Father made a stunning revelation.

The night started the same as usual, and nothing suggested that her Father had some news that might be of concern to her Mother and herself.

"Phyllis, dear, I would like you and Layla to join me in the library with our drinks. I need to discuss something with you, and I feel it would be better to keep it private for now."

Layla was intrigued by her Father's announcement, and the remainder of dinner seemed to take a long time as they went through the numerous courses and declined dessert.

When dinner finished, and the servants removed themselves from the library, Henry Buckingham steepled his fingers together before speaking.

"I have been thinking about our affairs and what happens to you, my dear, if I pass before you do."

Lady Buckingham looked stunned, and Layla inhaled sharply. Did her Father have an incurable disease or a life-threatening condition? Her Father chuckled.

"I see you have drawn incorrect conclusions from my opening statement. I am fit and hearty, but I believe it is foolish to leave things to chance. I don't want you, Phyllis, to be at the mercy of whoever inherits our estate. With no male heir, the nearest relative the courts can find will become the Earl, and another person or family will own all the entailed properties. I can set aside the funds, but it seems petty to allow someone else to inherit the estate and be unable to maintain it. Not only would the new Earl suffer, but our tenants would also suffer. That being the case, I have decided to purchase unentailed properties and accumulate extra funds."

A moment's silence followed Lord Buckingham's statement, and then Layla and her Mother seemed to regain their voices simultaneously. The following conversation was jumbled, and Lord Buckingham held up a hand to indicate they should stop talking.

"One at a time would be easier for me to answer your questions. You go first, Phyllis."

"Henry, dear, it is heartening to hear that I will not be destitute should you die before me. Pray, tell, how you intend to fund unentailed estates and accumulate money? What is your plan?"

"Ah, this is the tricky part. I know you aspire to be one of the most important hostesses in the ton, and those people despise trade, but that is what I intend to pursue."

Lady Buckingham looked as though she might swoon. All her good work at networking and cultivating the significant women of the ton would come to naught. She would be a pariah, ignored by all.

"Oh, goodness me, can you not make money another way? What good are riches if I have no social standing?"

Layla decided to shift the focus of the conversation.

"Father, what type of trade did you have in mind?"

"Ah, now that is what I wanted to discuss. I met a man at White's the other night, and despite not being a titled man or the offspring of titled parents, people, in most instances, accept him. So, hopefully, Phyllis, your ruination should be minimal. I met Sir George Fitzwilliam, who owns a suite of businesses. He holds a plantation in India and ships sugar and tobacco to Europe and England. While that is a challenging investment, it yields him significant rewards. I am not as adventurous as he is, and I am considering pursuing our trade between England and France. The Cornish fishermen smuggled rum into the country during the wars against the French. Now, the business is legal; we could ship rum, fabric, and other goods that the French manufacture. The shorter distance between England and France ought to minimise the risks."

Layla sat with her mouth gaping, and her mother continued to fan herself as though her swoon was imminent. Lord Buckingham said nothing, waiting for the women in his family to come to terms with what he said. In their defence, he had tossed around this idea for over a fortnight, so for them to accept his decision swiftly was unlikely. Other investment opportunities, such as the railways, were fraught with dangers, and more than one wealthy individual lost everything when the proposed railway took a different route or was cancelled altogether.

"Father, who owns the ships you would use, and how do you encourage trade? Is this Sir George Fitzwilliam honest? Does he have bookwork to back up his ventures?"

"I would own part of the ships until the profits allow me to purchase the vessel. I need George's assistance in generating trade partners, but his contacts will be invaluable, even though he trades with sugar and tobacco merchants. I will ask to see his books to reassure me that the proposition is viable."

"What happens if the ship is full of cargo and sinks?"

"My dear, I will have the ship and the cargo insured. The risk is minimal."

Layla rose and poured a snifter into three glasses.

"It looks like we are in business."

Layla and her father clinked glasses, but Lady Buckingham was more reserved; her doubts about the venture were clear to her husband, but he had to make the most likely decisions to protect his family if the need arose.

George Fitzwilliam became a frequent visitor as the two men worked through the details of the venture. Often, the men would take a break from their work to join the ladies. George was a great conversationalist, and Layla listened to his stories of world travel and his experiences on the Indian plantation with fascination. She could understand how her Father had become caught up in the excitement of doing something daring to bolster his funds. She hoped there would be no impediments to the venture; nothing could dim enthusiasm like a significant hold-up.

When questioned about his family, George described his wife and son, whom he loved dearly. He spoke in glowing terms of his son, and Layla hoped that the men weren't planning a meeting in the hopes that the two would be a match. A businessman who frequently travelled to many locations did not sound like a suitable husband for her. She wondered if she should caution her Father regarding her making a match with the Fitzwilliam son, but decided to leave well alone. If a match was not in the minds of the Father, her warning might have results she'd rather avoid.

Chapter Three

While her Father continued his deal with George Fitzwilliam, Layla and her Mother continued their endless round of social events. The longer the season continued, the more disheartened Layla became. Not one gentleman paid particular attention to her, and as the season progressed, many of her dance partners chose to court other debs. Layla wondered if her broken engagement last season was why no men saw her as a prospective wife. It was one thing to dance with a lady, but it was entirely different to court, and eventually, I married her. Did the men fear that Layla would humiliate them just as she had done to the Duke if they made their interests known?

After another unsuccessful night, Lady Buckingham voiced her disappointment to her husband.

"Everyone was so welcoming when the season started, and very few people mentioned the broken betrothal or Maggie's troubles, so I thought we were in the clear. While the men danced with Layla and chatted with her, none showed the slightest interest in pursuing her. I doubt a third season would help if what occurred last year is enough to discourage others from forming an attachment."

"I have a suggestion that I'm sure Layla will fight, but George speaks highly of his son; if we invite the family for dinner, will it look too much like a set-up to Layla?"

"I'm not sure what Layla will think, but at this point, we need all the help we can get. We have nothing to lose if the man does not measure up."

When her Mother told Layla of the proposed dinner, she grimaced.

"I wondered how long it would take to decide the Fitzwilliam man was worth a look. I hate that we have to resort to fake dinner invitations to see if the man would make a suitable husband."

"My dear, the dinner invitation is well overdue; with your Father and George working together on a venture, we should offer our hospitality to his wife and son."

Three evenings after their conversation, Lady Buckingham hosted the Fitzwilliam family. She had fussed over the menu and table setting for days, and for those not in the know, the level of preparation suggested the guests were royalty. The one aspect of the evening that Mother couldn't control was the absence of Beckett Fitzwilliam. Despite acknowledging and accepting the invitation, the much-lauded son did not arrive. George Fitzwilliam was embarrassed by his son's absence but excused his non-attendance with a tale about unexpected trouble with a shipment. Even though Beckett Fitzwilliam's absence put a pall over the beginning of the evening, by the time the guests finished their meal, all was well. Lady Buckingham and Lady Fitzwilliam had organised to meet for morning tea one day soon, and an invitation to join them for a meal would follow.

An incident overshadowed Layla's concern about meeting Beckett Fitzwilliam as she and Tilly walked to the park. Usually, the driver drove the ladies to the park, and after they strolled in the gardens, he returned them to the house. Today, however, one carriage horse had thrown a shoe, and rather than not enjoy the park, Layla and Tilly decided to walk. Anders, the driver, assured the ladies he would travel to the park to collect them as soon as he rectified the issue with the horse.

When the ladies set out, there was little traffic in their residential street, and with a footman following behind, they chatted and laughed. While Tilly was Layla's lady's maid, she was the only servant close in age to Layla, and with her contemporaries gone, Layla considered Tilly a friend. As they entered the park, there was a hold-up of carriages, and since they were on foot, they bypassed the bottleneck and continued along the path. They had barely begun their walk when the angry man from the modiste's accosted them.

"What the devil do you think you're doing?"

The footman who had trailed behind stepped in front of the ladies and scrutinised the tall, angry man.

"Sir, your conversation is offensive, and I urge you to take your unreasonable anger and depart."

He pushed past the footman, and his loud voice and menacing manner caused both girls to step back. When neither answered, he said, "What, cat got your tongue? I asked why you pushed your way through the lineup and entered the park before these people who arrived before you. You may have a bodyguard with you, but he won't stop the disdain from others you have pushed in front of."

Layla looked at Tilly and shrugged.

"Not that my actions have anything to do with you; we entered because we didn't have to manoeuvre a carriage or jostle for position. Once again, you behave in a bullying manner, and I wish to have no further dealings with you. Tilly and I will continue with our walk, and I would appreciate it if you would cease to speak."

As the girls moved away, Layla heard the man cursing about entitled little hussies and their footman's angry, frustrated voice. The man accosted them, and his anger had taken the shine out of the day. Although Layla and Tilly continued their walk, the pleasure had diminished.

When Anders arrived some minutes later, the girls ended their walk.

"I wonder who he is and why he bullies me?"

Tilly sighed. "It might be worth your Father making enquiries. If he constantly confronts you, you can't go about your business while expecting the worst."

The meal at the Fitzwilliams' house was fast approaching, and despite her initial reservations, Layla was looking forward to meeting Beckett

Fitzwilliam. But little did she know that the man in question had no intentions of meeting her, which caused consternation and anger with his parents.

"Beckett, I have invited the Buckinghams so they can meet you. We are now business partners, so you will see a lot of Henry Buckingham. It is better for business if you are friendly with the family."

"That may be so, but I refuse to be a patsy and pretend to be interested in an airhead who can't hold a conversation and giggles inanely. Rest assured, I will find a wife when the time comes, but your business partner's daughter will not be her. Have you done due diligence on the girl? She was engaged to a Duke, and when she ended it, there was much conversation about his dallying with others, which was supposed to be a deal breaker for her. Her sister killed the same Duke when he expressed interest in her, and she suddenly married an army Captain. Father, this family will not give you the social connection you wish to make, and even if they did, I would not court the girl."

George Fitzwilliam said, "Son, Cecilia did the wrong thing by you; nobody deserves to be jilted, but that doesn't mean all other debutantes are the same. You say you will marry when the time comes, but how do you anticipate finding a woman who isn't part of society? Do you intend to marry one of the demimondes or a barmaid? If that is the case, I will not approve."

Lady Fitzwilliam said, "Beckett, your description of the Buckingham daughter is so wrong it beggars belief. She is a pretty girl with a winning smile, and I swear I haven't heard her giggle inanely at any time. She can discuss world affairs and ask intelligent questions about the business venture. I like the girl very much."

Beckett gave his Mother a blank stare. "If you like the girl so much, I suggest you adopt her because that's the only way she will become part of our family. Now, I must ready myself for my evening."

George Becket watched his son walk away. "With that attitude, it's best he doesn't attend the dinner. I would hate to insult the Buckinghams because Beckett is surly and insulting. What did we do to deserve this level of contempt?"

Lady Fitzwilliam shook her head, but believing the question was rhetorical, she did not answer.

The dinner at Fitzwilliam's house was a great success. Layla liked the down-to-earth couple, and the conversation was lively and engaging. George Fitzwilliam made an excuse for Beckett's absence, but Layla suspected the reason was a ruse to cover up the man's reluctance to meet her family. If the son thought his parents intended to have them court, she could understand his reluctance to attend and find himself in a difficult situation. Layla had no intention of shoring up her Father's business deal by marrying the son, but if he had a backbone, could he not set his parents right and meet with the Buckinghams with a clear conscience?

Chapter Four

Layla begged off the following week's activities and journeyed to see Maggie. Her ability to skip the week's events firmed in Layla's mind, and her Mother's assessment of the poor quality of candidates and the unlikely arrival of gentlemen that might interest Layla allowed her to halt activity for a short while. Last season, Maggie and Layla had a falling out due to Layla's infatuation with a Duke and Maggie's mistrust of the gentleman. The events that unfolded during the season opened Layla's eyes to the type of man her fiancé was, and she ended their association. The sisters had repaired their relationship, and Layla was eager to see how Maggie was, as she was with child and unlikely to take any coach trips to visit her family during her confinement. Carriage trips, as a rule, were tedious and with Layla's excitement at a peak, this trip seemed to take longer than usual. When the coach entered the driveway of the Divine estate, Layla was ready to jump from the vehicle as soon as it stopped. Only her etiquette training and the restraining hand of her maid prevented her from jumping from the coach.

Much to Maxwell's disgust, Maggie greeted her sister and maid at the door, making the butler superfluous. Even though the girls had much to catch up on, Maggie insisted that Layla freshen up before they chatted. Once the footmen carried the trunks to Layla's room, Tilly walked to the kitchen while Layla settled in the sitting room.

"Where is the handsome captain?"

Maggie blushed with pleasure and said, "I expect he will have seen the carriage so that he won't be far away."

"Are you happy, Maggie? You don't regret the hasty wedding?"

Maggie glowed. "I do regret not having the white dress and the church full of guests, but the real reason people marry is so they can share their lives, and I couldn't be happier. I have a husband who loves me and a baby nearly ready to enter the world; what more could I want?"

Layla sighed. "I fear I will never have what you and Esme have. Even though the men chat and dance with me on social occasions, they are not serious contenders for marriage. Most of the men with titles are courting, much to Mother's disgust, and after being fooled last time, I'm reluctant to try again." After a long breath, she said, "No more woe is me; have you heard about Father's latest investment?"

As Layla informed Maggie about her Father's new business, her mind returned to Beckett Fitzwilliam. If she could send a message to him to assure him she was not hoping for a courtship, would he attend the next dinner? Maggie watched as her sister's mind wandered and raised an eyebrow at Layla.

"Where did you just go?"

After Layla explained her thoughts, Maggie agreed that sending a message to the man might be the simplest way to defuse the tension caused by his non-appearance. Layla suddenly remembered the man who bullied and shouted at her, but Theo Devine entered at that moment, and after kissing his wife, he kissed Layla's cheek before sitting next to Maggie.

"How goes it, little sister?"

Layla laughed. "Nobody told me having a big brother would be such fun. I feel sorry for you, Maggie. One day, I might marry, and I'll have a husband and a big brother, and you only have a husband."

Maggie smiled. "Trust me, Layla; you can have the big brother as long as I can have the husband."

Theo changed the subject when he asked Layla about the season. She repeated the information she had told Maggie, but the thought of the rude man came to mind.

"I recently encountered the rudest, most uncouth gentleman I have ever met."

Theo frowned when Layla finished recalling the accident outside the modiste's shop and the incident at the park.

"Have you told your Father about this man?"

"Yes, but there is no way to identify him because I haven't seen him at any events. Father now sends us out with a footman, and Jerry had to intervene at the park the other day. The man is so angry, insulting and rude, and I can't think what I have done to elicit a response like his."

"If he causes more trouble, it might be worth your Father contacting the Bow Street Runners to investigate the scoundrel."

"I hate to get the authorities involved, but I might have to ask Father to pursue the issue if I run across him again."

Pushing aside the unpleasant memories, Layla and Maggie continued chatting about their lives and shared acquaintances and friends. Layla knew that when she had to return to town and the continuous round of activities, her time with Maggie would be a lovely memory to recall when the social whirl became too much to handle.

As the carriage pulled up to the portico, Layla sighed. Tilly grinned at her mistress.

"You're not looking forward to the rest of the season, are you?"

"Tilly, tell me, is there another way of finding a husband instead of being paraded around like horses at Tattersall's?"

"For proper ladies like you, miss, I doubt it. For servants and commoners like me, we go to the local dances and the markets. I can't see your Mother agreeing to escort you to the market, and any man you found would be unacceptable."

When Jack opened the door and lowered the steps, Layla smiled.

"Thank you for your presence, Jack. I always feel safer with you riding with us."

Jack smiled, "You are welcome. A stint in the country and Lady Maggie's cook's pastries are well worth the ride."

Upon entering the house, Layla discovered her Mother in a flap.

"Where have you been? You were supposed to return yesterday, and we have a dinner invitation tonight that you have to attend."

"Mother, we agreed that I would return today, and if you feel stressed about the invitation, why didn't you refuse?"

"Refuse? Are you mad? Lady Fitzwilliam is having a dinner party, and your father is eager to meet others and diversify their funds. While Tilly unpacks your trunks, I will summon the footmen to prepare a bath for you. Choose your nicest gown; I won't have us shaming your Father."

Tilly and Layla looked at each other in amazement. The girls walked through the hallway to Layla's room before Layla spoke.

"Shaming my Father? When have I ever dressed inappropriately and shamed my Father? I do believe my Mother is going batty."

The conversation ceased when the footmen placed the large tub on the floor in Layla's room, and when the pails of water filled the tub, Layla prepared for her bath. Never before had she seen her Mother in such a state, and she feared that her Father's business interests were not the only reason Lady Buckingham told Tilly to turn her mistress out well or heaven help her. Tilly was accustomed to Lady Buckingham's threats, and for the most part, she went about her business, fulfilling the job the family had hired her to do. Whether the event was prestigious or not, Tilly prided herself on always turning Layla out well.

Layla sat in the dressing chair as Tilly fiddled with her hair.

"This invitation seems more important than a business dinner. Do you think the prodigal son is attending, and I am supposed to swoon and fall into his arms?"

Tilly giggled. "You might be right, but be strong and hold out against his charms until dessert."

Layla snorted in an unladylike manner. Goodness knows what her Mother and Lady Fitzwilliam had in the works. Beckett Fitzwilliam might be a wise trader, but his manners were not as well polished as his business insight. A man who accepted an invitation but didn't attend and ignored requests from his family to meet new business partners was not a man Layla wanted to know. If the man arrived tonight, she would smile politely but in no way encourage him. Still, she had already informed her Mother that she wouldn't marry to further her Father's business interests, so she would be disappointed if that were her intention.

Chapter Five

As the butler opened the door, Layla and Lady Buckingham entered before Lord Buckingham. The butler led the small party towards the parlour, where visitors socialised and sipped drinks. Layla couldn't see Sir George or Lady Fitzwilliam in attendance, but assumed they were not far away. Father introduced his wife and Layla to a few acquaintances, and the guests turned as their hosts arrived. People exchanged greetings, and when Sir George made his way towards her Father, his expression was jovial. Layla liked the Fitzwilliams and had no trouble smiling at them and thanking them for their invitation.

The butler appeared and announced that dinner was ready, and Layla wondered what excuse the son would have tonight for not attending this dinner party. When the parlour door opened, a gentleman who introduced himself to Layla offered his arm to escort her to dinner. Sir George placed his hand on the arm of the newcomer and strode towards Layla.

"Miss Layla, I want you to meet my son. You must have wondered if he was a figment of my imagination."

Layla turned towards the newcomer, and after a shocked silence, the only word she could utter was "You." She stepped hastily away from the man and said, "I have met your son, Sir George. It seems we don't see eye to eye."

When Layla stepped back another few steps, she collided with her Mother, who had come to see the introduction. The bright smile she had on her face before the introduction turned to a frown, and she glared at Layla.

"I'm sure you can put aside your differences. What do you think, Sir Beckett?"

The man looked down his nose at Lady Buckingham and said, "I doubt it. Your daughter must be one of the most annoying women I've ever met."

Her Mother's gasp was only outdone by that of the guests. Sir George looked mortified, but the cad Beckett looked unperturbed. Layla stepped towards the door and fled, unsure where to go but confident she needed to be away from the horrid man. Who could have imagined that the surly, angry stranger belonged to Sir George and Lady Fitzwilliam, two of the nicest people she had ever met?

Layla opened doors until she found the library, and with the roaring fire and the muted candlelight, she crawled into an armchair and wept. Would this altercation ruin her Father's business deals? Her Mother had warned Layla not to shame her Father, but who could have predicted the cutting words of Beckett Fitzwilliam? Was she supposed to stand there and allow the man to insult her? When Layla ceased shaking and crying, she couldn't decide what to do. Would her parents come looking for her, or would she have to swallow her pride, enter the parlour, and look for them? Dinner must have finished, and Layla realised she was famished. She hoped this night would soon come to a close, and with that thought in her mind, she looked towards the door with anticipation. The smile on her face died as she faced her enemy. Beckett looked at the red-eyed woman sitting on the settee with disdain. He sneered at her puffy eyes and crumpled dress, but before he could make any insulting remarks, Layla said,

"Get out of here. If someone catches us together, you will ruin me, and we'll have to marry. Leave, please. Whatever you have to say can be said another time."

"I'll leave when I'm good and ready. I want to ensure that you understand there will be no marriage between us. When I marry, it won't be to a silly little girl with no original thoughts. I don't want a pampered princess; I need a partner, not a parasite."

By this time, Layla was weeping, both from the comments made by Beckett and the fear of being discovered.

"Please, please leave. Someone will come, and you will have to marry me, whether we like it or not."

"Nobody would dare enter the main body of the house except you because you seem to think you are so special that the rules don't apply to you."

The sound of the door opening made Layla wail, and even though the arrogant man in front of her thought he was safe to insult her with no consequences, he was proven wrong.

"What is going on in here? You, Sir Beckett, left an age ago, so we can only assume you two have been here, unchaperoned, for quite some time. Miss Layla can't stand to have her reputation further tarnished."

At this pronouncement, Layla's weeping turned into sobs and the stunned expression of his parents and the Buckinghams registered with Beckett. Regardless of his feelings for this girl, she would soon be his wife. With a feral growl, he stalked to the door and pushed through the crowd of onlookers. Tonight might be the night to hide out in his townhouse and consume the bottle of rum he had from his last trip. Tomorrow would be soon enough to deal with the problem the damned woman caused. He wouldn't have lost his temper and confronted her if she weren't so entitled and precious.

While Lady Buckingham escorted Layla to the carriage, Sir George and Henry Buckingham discussed their children's predicament. Lady Fitzwilliam had retired to the parlour with a stiff drink, aware that whatever their children's thoughts on the matter, the marriage was inevitable. When George introduced them earlier, it was evident from Layla's reaction that something had happened to make her wary of Beckett. And as much as it hurt her to admit it, she was sure that Beckett was the instigator of the friction between the two. If they had met before, as they had revealed, and Beckett had voiced the same opinions to her as he had to George and her, Layla had every right to want to put distance between them.

When George entered the parlour, he collected a glass and the decanter and sat beside his wife.

"What a mess. And even though Beckett is my son, I feel sorry for Layla. I don't know when they met, but if he shared his thoughts about her with us, it's no wonder she was distrustful of him. He has compromised her, and her reputation won't survive another hit; he must do the right thing by the girl."

Lady Fitzwilliam shook her head. "She may prefer to live out in the country rather than marry a man who hates her. This mess is all down to that hussy, Cecilia. Beckett has never recovered from being jilted by the woman he thought was his life partner, but it doesn't give him the right to bully another woman. He could grow to like her if he gave her a chance, but he is determined to cast all debutantes in the same mould as Cecilia."

George frowned. "Maybe he will be kinder to her when they are living together. Beckett needs to realise that she is as much a victim as he is, more so, probably because I can't imagine she invited him into the library after she excused herself and ran to hide at the commencement of the meal."

Chapter Six

Layla sat transfixed as Tilly fiddled with her hair and straightened her dress. Despite begging her parents not to force her to marry Beckett Fitzwilliam, Layla had no luck. Her Father was furious with her proposed spouse, but even though he realised her marriage would be unpleasant, he agreed with her Mother that Layla's reputation couldn't survive another scandal. Today was the day she was to marry the bounder, and try as she might, each time reality surfaced, the tears fell.

"Miss Layla, it is time."

Layla looked beseechingly at her maid.

"Promise me you will come to be my maid at my new home. I couldn't bear it if I were alone with that cad."

Tilly nodded. "I spoke to your Mother about moving; she thought it was a good idea. Now, come along. Your Father will be waiting for you."

Layla met her Father at the top of the stairs. He hooked her arm through his and said, "I am sorry and angry about that cad compromising you. What the devil was he thinking? I advise you to do your best to avoid him if he continues to be rude and makes offensive remarks."

Layla nodded mutely and walked to the parlour with her Father.

Layla wept as she stood beside Beckett, and the minister read the marriage ceremony. This farce was not how her marriage was supposed to happen; Layla wanted a man who would care for her and who she liked, not a man she hated and who, in return, hated her. Layla gulped and stuttered when asked if she took Beckett as her husband. And then, the ceremony was over, and she was married to a man she hated. The clergyman said that Beckett could kiss the bride, and he shuddered, saying, "I think not."

Layla's face flamed a bright red, and she ducked her head so the assembled guests couldn't see her distress.

Lady Fitzwilliam gasped at her son's insult and shook her head. "I fear that Layla has a hard road ahead of her."

George Fitzwilliam nodded. Words failed him; how could his son publicly treat his new wife so shamefully?

There was no celebration breakfast after the wedding, and once the footmen loaded her trunks, Layla and Tilly entered the carriage, and the journey to her new home began. After her stressful morning and the trauma of the wedding service, Layla was so exhausted that she fell asleep almost immediately. Tilly watched her mistress as she slept, glad that, for the moment, Layla could forget the night to come. Tilly was unsure whether the horrid man would decide to consummate the marriage, and she feared that if he did, he would complete the task as fast and brutally as he could. After all, why would he suddenly change his mind about his wife and be considerate when completing the bedding?

When the vehicle stopped at the front of the manor house, Beckett called home, and the outriders and their master were already there. Once the carriage reached the road where the house was located, the outriders and their master abandoned the vehicle as they cantered for home. Layla wondered what she was supposed to do as the footmen threw their trunks to the ground and headed into the house with them. When the new mistress arrived at any typical home, the staff would be lined up, ready to meet her. The absence of staff suggested she would not receive the respect she deserved.

Standing in the foyer, with no servants in attendance, Layla wondered where she and Tilly were to go. Noises from the back of the house drew Layla, and when she pushed the door, she discovered the servants seated at a long table preparing to eat. The butler noticed her first and sprang to his feet.

"Ma'am, what can I do for you? Sir Beckett didn't tell me he would have a companion."

"That would be because he didn't bring a companion; he brought his wife. My maid and I have had a long day and would appreciate it if somebody could show me to my room."

Layla thought the butler looked like he might swoon, but he regained his composure quickly.

"My apologies, Ma'am. Ella can show you to your room, and your maid can join us when you settle. Mrs Gardener will make you a tray in your room if that pleases you."

Layla and Tilly followed the housekeeper from the kitchen toward a long hallway. A runner ran the length of the hallway, and its frayed edges and the dust coating the hallway furniture suggested that while the house appeared to have an entire staff, most of them did the very least they could get away with. Tilly raised her eyebrows at Layla, and her mistress nodded slightly. One of the first jobs tomorrow was to discuss the lack of cleanliness of the house with the housekeeper.

When Mrs Gardener opened the bedroom door, Layla was pleased that the room seemed clean.

"Sir Beckett's room is through the connecting door, ma'am. If you need anything else, please don't hesitate to ask. I will send up a tray shortly and wish you a goodnight."

The housekeeper left the room, and Tilly laughed.

"I love how the upper servants pretend to be superior, but by the look of this house, she is either inept at her job or doesn't care. The house is a disgrace, but I noticed the staff were tucking into a veritable feast in the kitchen."

"Yes, I imagine it will be my job to sort out the mess. Beckett has his nose stuck in the air, so I doubt he has realised his staff is taking advantage.

Layla sat on the dressing chair, surveying her surroundings. She was unsure whether to climb into bed or wait for her husband, assuming he intended to consummate the marriage, where she was. With a shrug, Layla climbed into bed and snuffed out the candle. She hadn't seen the horrid man since they arrived, and she certainly was not going to look for him to ask about his intentions. Noises from the next room made her stomach clench as she imagined him getting ready for bed. Esme and Maggie said that the intimate aspect of marriage was one of the best ways a couple could express their feelings, and they also noted that if the man was skilled and genuinely cared about his wife, the experience could be enjoyable for both of them. The problem with all those lovely words was that while Layla imagined her new husband had the skill to help her enjoy the experience, he hated her and would hardly be kind in fulfilling his duty.

Layla was startled when the connecting door burst open, and her husband strode into the room. He held a candle in his hand, and when he reached the bed, he pushed it into the sconce on the wall and approached her. The angry look on his face terrified Layla, and she knew nothing would be nice about what would happen. She lay in bed, silently observing her husband, and watched as a sneer appeared on his face.

"I have to consummate this farce of a marriage. Pull up your night rail to your waist and open your legs."

When Layla failed to follow his instructions, his sneer grew.

"Didn't your Mother tell you you must submit to my advances?"

Beckett reached down and ripped Layla's nightrail from her body. As she tried to cover herself, Beckett slid onto the bed.

"Don't worry about covering yourself. You are so ugly it might be hard for me to do my duty, but if I close my eyes, I might manage."

Layla gasped as she felt something cold applied roughly to the junction between her legs, and then a most painful invasion stopped her breath. Layla clawed at Beckett's arms, trying to get him to release her, but he persisted. Layla started to moan as her husband pushed further in, and the last thrust that felt like she was on fire elicited a scream. Layla had never experienced such pain; it felt like her insides were being ripped out. Layla cried, begging him to stop, and suddenly he abandoned her and she felt something warm and wet squirt on her stomach. Sobbing hysterically, Layla watched as Beckett rose from the bed and grabbed the washcloth from the basin, using it to clean himself. He dipped the cloth again, threw it at Layla and said, "Clean yourself, woman. If you were someone else, I might be happy to see you covered in my seed, but with you, I withdrew, so you can't get with child. I have done my duty, but I will never touch you again, and you can live in this grand house as a shrivelled-up spinster."

The door slamming behind her husband released fresh tears, and Layla used the wet cloth to wipe the sticky mess from her stomach. She needed to rinse the rag to finish cleaning herself, but doubted that her shaky legs would carry her to the washbasin, even if she could locate it in the dark. Using the sheet to remove the remainder of the sticky mess from her stomach, Layla curled into a ball and cried herself to sleep.

In his bedchamber, Beckett listened to the sound of his unwanted wife weeping. He felt a slight pang of guilt for the rough way he handled her, but his anger needed a release, so she bore the brunt of his rage. Beckett had never been a selfish lover, but even though his bride was a maiden, he could find no compassion for her tonight and doubted that he ever would. His messed-up life was her fault, and he intended to make her regret ever forcing him into this marriage.

Chapter Seven

When Tilly entered Layla's bed chamber the following day, she gasped. Layla sat on the edge of the bed, weeping; the red eyes and the destroyed night rail told the story of what had occurred the night before.

"Dear God, the man is an animal."

"Tilly, I hurt everywhere. Can you ask the footman to prepare a bath? I will sit behind the screen while they bring it in. I want to scrub the smell and the feel of that man from my skin, and while I bathe, will you ask the maids to change the bed linen?"

"Yes, I can do that, but your pain will be there for everyone to see."

Layla hung her head. "Do I look too bad?"

"Yes, but I'll use all my skills to turn you out so well that everyone will think all is well."

Beckett finally emerged from his study, and the attitude of the servants confused him. What had he done to make everyone look down their noses at him or give him disgusted looks? The answer to his dilemma came late in the afternoon when he entered the sitting room for refreshments and found his wife with red, swollen eyes.

"Are you going to sit there and blubber for weeks on end? I did what I had to, and now you can consider yourself a married woman."

Layla looked at her husband in shock. She shook her head in amazement and said, " Being raped by my husband on my wedding night will go down in history as one of the worst things that has ever happened to me. Discovering that you lack finesse and compassion when bedding a maiden was shocking. You say you will never bed me, so there will be no children from this marriage that you caused to happen; it suits me fine. I will stab or shoot you if you try to enter my room again."

Beckett stood immobile, the shock of her words showing on his face. His wife's uncharacteristic tongue-lashing stabbed at his conscience, raising the guilt he felt last night after taking her so roughly.

When Beckett stormed from the room, Layla watched in horror. How was she to endure a lifetime of marriage to this bully? Layla would have taken the second option if her parents had given her the choice of marriage to Beckett or banishment to the country. In both her marriage and potential exile, she would never have children of her own, but at least in the country, she wouldn't have to suffer the bullying behaviour of her husband. Considering the marriage was his fault, couldn't he manage a trace of civility?

Layla stood up; she could sit here and wallow in her misery or call the housekeeper to discuss the poor standard of housework. She may have to live with an ogre, but she didn't have to live in a filthy home. Layla's conversation with Mrs Gardner didn't go as planned because the woman defended the level of cleanliness in the house, and her attitude towards Layla was less than respectful. When the woman walked away, her cocky demeanour rankled with Layla. She decided she might have to live with a bully, but she would not tolerate disrespect. She contemplated the measures she could take and asked Ellis to send Tilly into the sitting room; her maid was always practical, and she might suggest how to deal with the housekeeper.

After much discussion, it became apparent that Layla would have to let the woman go. But finding a replacement would be tricky and time-consuming. Layla chuckled to herself; time was something she had plenty of. She penned a letter to her Mother explaining the situation and asking for suggestions for a replacement. While sending letters would not resolve the problem immediately, the woman, unbeknownst to her, was on borrowed time.

Avoiding her husband while finding something worthwhile to do kept Layla busy for the day, but she knew she couldn't remain in hiding for the rest of her life. The days of inactivity and avoidance became Layla's lot, even though she chaffed at the lack of worthwhile tasks. The only time she sat down to a meal with Beckett, his insults and verbal abuse were so severe that she lost her appetite and retired without dinner.

Within three weeks of the beginning of her marriage, Beckett spent more and more time away from the house. Layla breathed a sigh of relief on the nights he didn't return, but his desertion annoyed her because she could not leave the house while he was away. Maybe she could ask him to buy another carriage with a driver at her disposal so she and Tilly could visit. Layla was furious the morning Sir Beckett returned and instructed his valet to pack his trunks. The horrid man who had forced her into marriage was moving to another residence. Layla tackled her husband about this new track their marriage was taking.

"Sir Beckett, as you haven't got the manners to inform me of your movements, am I to assume you are moving out of this house?"

Beckett barely looked at Layla as he continued to pack his belongings.

"I fail to see what business it is of yours where I live. Did you think I would be content to rusticate in this house, constantly being annoyed by your presence? I don't have to justify my movements to you, but yes, I am moving house. My mistress and I will live in a new residence I have purchased. You can do what you please."

"Who will pay for the upkeep of this house?"

Beckett roared at Layla, and she stepped away, terrified that he might hit her.

"You grasping, lying hussy, that's all you're worried about? You damned entitled debutantes think of nothing but your comfort and the wealth of the poor cad who marries you. I will do my husbandly duties and support you; what you do with your life is not my concern."

Beckett's forcefulness shook Layla, but she refused to be cowed by the man.

"I might send a letter of sympathy to your mistress. What a sad life she lives, being mauled by you whenever the urge takes you. No woman should have to endure what I did, and even if you pay her well, she must have a miserable life."

Beckett laughed, but there was no humour in the sound.

"If you were a real woman, you might enjoy the ministrations of a man."

"You're right; I might enjoy the ministrations of a man, but trust me, no woman would enjoy being assaulted, which is what you did to me."

Layla fled from the room, determined to forget the hurtful things her husband spewed at her.

Chapter Eight

Life settled after Beckett's desertion, and when her Mother's letter arrived, Layla was eager to read what she had to say. She waded through the goings-on of her parents and their acquaintances, and as the letter continued, Layla began to feel that her mother had not taken the time to deal with her problem. When she turned the page, it was evident that her Mother had left what Layla considered most important to last. Her Mother gave her the names of two ladies looking for a placement, each with references from their previous employers. The reason for their unemployment became apparent when her Mother explained that one of the women had to return home to a sick relative, who sadly had died. The second was the housekeeper for Lord Aningdale, and the man died without issue, so the courts allowed the staff to go while they searched for an heir.

Buoyed by the news of possible placements, Layla responded to her mother, requesting that she arrange for these women to visit her home. The thought that she could fire the lazy woman who called herself a housekeeper was a relief. Layla decided that if she were the primary occupant of the house, she would make her own decisions regarding the running of the place. A week later, when her Mother wrote giving her the arrival details of the candidates, Layla called Ellis to the sitting room.

"Ellis, as the head of the staff, I want to inform you that two women are arriving tomorrow to interview for the housekeeper's job. I trust you to keep this information confidential. Until I have spoken to the women, I don't know if either will be a good fit for our home, and the last thing I need is more confrontations."

As Ellis left the room, he gave nothing away regarding the news, but she felt confident that he would keep the information to himself.

The following day, the women arrived separately, and as Layla interviewed the first candidate, the second sat in the parlour with Tilly. Layla liked the first candidate, and when the second woman entered the room, she felt uncomfortable under her scrutiny. Although Layla had already decided on the first woman, she wanted to be fair to both as they had travelled quite a distance. Much to her dismay, the woman asked questions that Layla felt were inappropriate and when she called the candidate on her questions, the woman became belligerent.

"I have worked in respectable households and don't want to tarnish my reputation by working for someone with a scandal surrounding them. If your husband doesn't live here, where does he live?"

Layla stood and walked to the door.'

"Ellis, please escort this busybody out, and then you can ask Mrs Hogkin to return to the sitting room."

Once Ellis pushed the protesting woman from the house, Layla laughed. Tilly and Mrs Hogkin found Layla doubled over with laughter, and they stood staring at her for a moment while she regained control.

"Dear me, that would be like jumping from the frying pan into the fire. That woman wasn't only nosy, but she was also disrespectful. Mrs Hogkin, I would be pleased to offer you the housekeeper job, but I feel compelled to tell you that much work is needed to bring the cleanliness up to scratch."

"Lady Fitzwilliam, I must confess that I have studied the rooms I have seen and concur. But we will work hard and clean your place thoroughly."

"I will ask Tilly to keep you company, and I'd offer refreshments, but when I tell the current housekeeper I am letting her go, I fear the woman will throw the food, not deliver it."

Layla's assessment of Mrs Gardner's reaction to her dismissal was accurate. At first, the woman refused to believe Layla would let her go, but then she became belligerent.

"You can't replace me; you don't pay me; Sir Beckett does. He is the only one who can fire me, not you. We all know you are his pretend wife, and I don't have to take orders from you."

"Mrs Gardner, why don't you take this problem up with Sir Beckett? Ah, that's right, he doesn't live here any more, so the hiring and firing is my job. You have thirty minutes to collect your things and the wages owing. If you are not off the property within the hour, I will ask the footmen to remove you."

The woman grumbled about Layla but then rallied.

"You won't find anyone to replace me. You must act as the housekeeper because no one else will do the job."

"Mrs Garner, I have already hired your replacement. Now get moving, or you will leave the property without your belongings."

Layla watched as the woman disappeared up the stairs and waited for her to return with her belongings. Ellis pulled out his purse, dolled out some coins, and then sent her on her way. When the woman vacated the house, Layla addressed the servants.

"I am the mistress of this house. If taking orders from me is objectionable, it would be best if you left now. If you stay, you will work with Mrs Hogkin, our new housekeeper, instead of sitting around and eating more than your fair share of the food in this house. I will expect you to earn your keep. Does anyone else want to leave?"

When there were no replies, Layla told Ellis to come and meet the housekeeper so that he could introduce her to the staff.

Chapter Nine

Within a week, the rooms that had previously been dusty and grimy now shone. Having spent the week choosing menus and replacing broken items, Layla felt a sense of satisfaction, but the problem of her isolation remained. Beckett had taken the carriage and the driver, so Layla was confined to the house. She didn't know how to contact him, and she couldn't go and plead her case without a horse to ride. She knew that Sir George and Lady Fitzwilliam lived nearby, and she decided that if all else failed, she would ride there to ask for assistance. With a formulated plan, Layla ventured outside to the stables. The smell of mouldy hay and manure made her screw up her nose, and she realised that the stable hands were managing their tasks poorly. Did Beckett never check on his servants, or was he too busy tupping his mistress to see what was before his nose? Layla entered the building and had the overwhelming desire to cover her nose with her kerchief. The building looked empty, except for the horses who inquisitively looked over their stable doors. Layla ventured further into the building and found a group of men playing cards at a table. The men looked up but stayed seated.

"What do you want?"

"A little respect would be good, and then some answers. You will address me as Lady Fitzwilliam, and I need to know who is in charge here?"

"I am in charge here, and I answer to Sir Beckett, not you."

Layla laughed. "The former housekeeper said the same thing, and I sent her packing. Unless you are remarkably unobservant, Sir Beckett is not here, nor has he been here for quite some time. I need to know which of these horses is suitable for me to ride."

The head groom scowled at Layla before snapping, "None of these horses takes a side saddle, so none of them would be suitable as a lady's mount."

"And as the head groom, are you incapable of training the quietest of these animals to take a side saddle? I'm surprised my husband hires staff who aren't capable of doing their jobs. If I have my own mount brought here, I will require a groom to ride with me."

"We don't have time to look after another mount, and my men are not babysitters. We will not be accompanying you on a stroll around the grounds."

Layla stalked away from the stables, disgusted that the oaf could claim too much work when four men were tending to four horses, none of which she had seen exercised or their stables cleaned. As Layla walked back to the house, she mulled over the best way to tackle the problem of the stables and the horses. When Ellis opened the front door for her, she said, "Before our marriage, how often did Sir Beckett visit the estate?"

"My Lady, Sir Beckett lived here during the off-season."

"So he knows about his lazy employees, or has he never ventured as far as the stables? The stalls and the surrounding yard are putrid, and the stench is appalling. The four men tasked with tending to the four horses have hunkered down, playing cards, and they tell me they are either unable or unwilling to train a horse to side saddle. Can the man be so oblivious to the state of his property?"

"I'm sorry the staff don't meet your standards, Lady Fitzwilliam. Perhaps a note sent to his lordship might address the problem."

"That would be amazing, Ellis, except I don't know where Sir Beckett lives. Do you know?"

Ellis shook his head. "I'm sorry, my lady, but I don't know either."

"Maybe I should contact Sir George? He must know where Sir Beckett is; if he doesn't, he might be able to deal with the stable hands because they deem it beneath themselves to deal with the mistress of the house."

Later that morning, Layla pulled out a sheet of paper, and as she debated what to say to Sir George, a commotion at the front door announced the arrival of her wayward spouse. Beckett shattered the house's calm as he shouted instructions and loud orders at the staff who attempted to manhandle his trunk and ran to fulfil his demands. Layla sighed; the arrival of her husband made the note to Sir George redundant, and she hoped that when he stopped shouting orders, she might have a conversation about the stables.

Once the chaos of her husband's arrival dimmed, Layla asked Mrs Hogkin to alert the cook that, with Sir Beckett arriving, dinner needed to have more selections than she regularly chose. Laya was sure that if she presented him with the one meal option she had partaken of, he would criticise her and demean her ability to run the house. When Layla arrived for dinner, Ellis pulled out her chair and seated her as Becket watched with a scowl.

"I'm amazed at how useless former debutantes are. Can you not sit in a chair without a servant's help?"

Layla briefly gazed at her husband.

"Is your mistress expected to seat herself without your assistance? The woman chose poorly if you show no manners when dealing with other ladies."

The meal continued in silence until Beckett slammed his utensils down.

"Why must I endure your presence as I eat my meal? I never want to see you, and sitting at your table is torture. Your presence reminds me of how you trapped me in this marriage."

Layla looked at the servers.

"Please select foods for Sir Beckett and move his place setting to the breakfast room."

The servers gaped at Layla's decree but hastily followed her request when Sir Beckett rose from the table. As he stalked away, Layla smirked. If he wanted to arrive unannounced and act like an ass, she could give back as much aggravation as he could.

That night, Layla checked that she had locked the door between her room and her husband's. She didn't think he would try to force his attention on her again, but she wasn't taking any chances. The sound of male voices in the next room was unusual because she usually was alone in the upstairs section of the house at night. It amazed her that Beckett blamed her for the marriage when, in fact, it was his fault. If he had listened to her warnings instead of being his entitled, arrogant self, neither of them would be in a marriage they didn't want. How often did he intend to visit the estate, and how long would he stay? Layla resolved to speak to her husband the next day about the groom and the stable hands. She couldn't force the staff to show her respect, but she could terminate their employment if they weren't doing their jobs. The state of the stalls and the barn showed that they weren't doing much, except playing cards and collecting their wages.

When Layla reached the breakfast room, Beckett was finishing his breakfast. The disgusted look he gave her should have made Layla angry, but she couldn't afford to antagonise her husband because she needed to talk with him about the stable hands. Before he could leave the room, Layla said, "My Lord, I need to discuss an issue regarding the estate, and I hoped to do that when I finished my breakfast."

Beckett glared at his wife. "The running of the estate has nothing to do with you, and I doubt anything you have to say would be worth my attention."

"Sir Beckett, you should spare me the time to discuss an issue unless you want to argue and have the servants as the audience."

Beckett cast a disgusted look at Layla and grunted as he walked away. Layla assumed the grunt was an agreement to speak, and even if it wasn't, she intended to have her say regarding the stables.

Layla knocked on the study door after finishing breakfast, then pushed it open. She wasn't delusional enough to think her husband would ask her to enter. Beckett towered over her as Layla sat in the armchair closest to his desk.

"What do you want?"

"My Lord, I have a question before I tell you my concern. When was the last time you entered the stables?"

"What kind of stupid question is that?"

"A question that needs an answer, but true to form, you will not make an intelligent decision, so I will make it easy for you. Yesterday, I went to the stables to see if there was a mount that I could ride. It took me a few minutes to find your staff because they were playing cards in the back room. The stables and the barn reeked of mouldy hay and manure, and the grooms were most disrespectful. I wanted a horse to ride and a groom to accompany me, but they refused to break a horse to the side saddle and said they were not employed to babysit."

"And what am I supposed to do?"

Layla gasped. "You're the damned boss; I expect you to tell them to clean the stables and the barn and find a horse for me to ride. I need a groom to ride with me, and as they seem to be doing nothing, I don't think it's too much to ask."

"As I leave, I will go via the stables and speak with the head groom."

"Thank you."

Chapter Ten

Beckett left the following day without as much as a by-your-leave, and Layla was once again alone in the mansion. She wanted to ride and wished Tilly could go with her, but Tilly insisted that if the driver hadn't hitched the horse to a carriage, she had no business approaching it. Feeling restless, Layla went to the stables. If Beckett had spoken to the stable lads and grooms, they had taken no heed of his warnings.

"What do you want, missy?"

"We already had that discussion; I am Lady Fitzwilliam to you. Sir Beckett said he would speak to you about the filth in the stables and that you are providing a groom to escort me when I go riding."

"Sir Beckett never came to the stables and didn't say we have to babysit you. Besides, there is no horse for you to ride, so the problem of someone riding with you is not an issue."

Layla was furious as she left the stables. Beckett had said he would speak to the grooms, but she wondered why she thought he would follow through. If the problem related to Beckett, he would address it, but he couldn't care less where she was concerned. When she arrived at the house, she asked Ellis to send Tilly to the drawing room and to ask Mrs Hogkin for refreshments for them. Ellis gave her a sidelong glance, and she bristled.

"Ellis, do you see any ladies visiting me?"

"Ah, no, my lady."

"Do you see me jaunting off to have morning tea with the society ladies?"

"Ah, no, maám."

"I have known Tilly since we were girls, and my Father sent her with me so I would have company. She is my only friend, and even if I wanted to socialise with the ladies of the ton, I have no transportation. Your illustrious employer took the carriage, and without a suitable horse from the stables to ride, I am stranded and alone. So get used to seeing me with Tilly."

"Certainly, maám."

Tilly arrived with the tea tray, and Layla nodded when she asked if she should pour.

"It scandalised the staff that you and I should take tea, but as I pointed out to Ellis, you are my only companion. When my husband made a short visit to check that I hadn't sold the silver goblets or some other such rubbish, I spoke to him about the filth in the stables, the lack of activity from his so-called staff and their refusal to break something to side saddle for me. If they had done some work riding, one of the four mounts would have been feasible, but then I would need a groom to accompany me, and they refused. Beckett said he would speak to them, but he didn't. Why put yourself out for the woman you forced into an unwanted marriage? He might think he is hard done by, but he should trade places with me for a while."

"Miss Layla, your Father sent me so you had company when it became clear that Sir Beckett intended to be hateful, so why not see if he would send Dancer here?"

"If Dancer were here, I could ride, but the grooms would claim they have too much work to do, and they would neglect her."

"Write to your Father and tell him your concerns; he might send a stable boy with Dancer."

Two weeks later, the sound of hooves on the driveway lured Layla to the front windows—the sight before her gladdened her heart. Racing through the house, she called out. "Tilly, Tilly, Dancer is here."

Layla stepped out onto the driveway with a smile that lit her face, and then she stopped with shock. A young boy rode Dancer, but a familiar face accompanied him.

"Jack, oh my gosh, Jack. It's so good to see a friendly face."

Against all protocol, Layla hugged her bodyguard, who had become a jack-of-all-trades once the danger caused by a mad nobleman had disappeared. The break in etiquette shocked both the young lad and Ellis, but Layla didn't give a fig. Tilly joined them, and her smile reflected her joy at seeing her friend. The boy riding Dancer slid from the saddle, and Layla reached for her horse.

"You can't know how much I missed you," she told her horse.

She returned to the riders and said, "You must be tired and hungry. I'd suggest putting the horses in the stables, but they are putrid. Let's turn them out in the paddock, and we can decide what to do after you rest."

She squeezed Jack's arm and said, "You'd better go around to the kitchen; otherwise, my staff will rebel and desert me if I bring you in the front door."

Jack grinned, and as he and his young companion disappeared, Layla grabbed Tilly and did a most unladylike jig.

"Remind me to write to my Father and tell him how much I love him. He could have sent anyone with Dancer, but to send Jack was a kindness I won't forget. I wonder how long he can stay?"

That evening, Tilly and Layla shared their concern about the state of the stables with Jack. As a bodyguard, he had often watched over Layla and Maggie during the trying time that was their first season, but this evening was the first time he had shared a table with them. Layla was confident that the other servants were scandalised, but was it her fault that her two best friends were not of the gentry? Tonight, Jack and the young stable boy, Max, would sleep in the servants' quarters, but when Jack left, Max would sleep in the stables. How could she allow a young boy to sleep in such filth?

"We will have to clean a stall for Dancer, and I suggest that Max sleeps next to her. First thing tomorrow, he and I will clean what we can. I don't like the sound of the blighters your vile husband has employed, but we'll do our best."

The following morning, Tilly and Layla arrived at the stables. Angry voices rang out, and Layla hurried to discover the cause. It amazed her to find the stable hands shouting at Jack and Max. The argument looked like there would be no quick resolution, so Layla sidled up to Jack and pulled his gun from the waistband of his breeches. She fired a shot in the air, and the loud sound shocked the combatants into silence. Layla pointed the gun at the stable hands.

"You'd better behave because I don't have much practice with a gun; I just might shoot you by accident."

Jack grinned and held his hand out for the weapon, and Layla handed it to him, butt first. It seemed she did know a little about guns.

"Now, you lazy, nothing. I asked my Father to send my horse, and he also sent Max, who will look after Dancer, as you gentlemen are so busy with the four mounts here. Max will need to sleep in the stables, and I would not ask my worst enemy to sleep in this filth. Jack and Max are here to clean a stable for Dancer and a place for Max to sleep, although Max will have to suffer the stench, considering the rotting hay and manure in the rest of the stables. You have nothing to do, so go back and play cards, twiddle your thumbs, or whatever you do to keep you busy while you do no work."

The grooms and headman could find nothing to grumble about, as the addition of another horse that they didn't have to care for would not impact them. As the men walked away, Jack was concerned for the welfare of the horse, the boy, and his mistress. Once the two stalls were clean, Layla and Jack went for a ride. It was great to have her horse here; the company she shared made the ride even better. Jack knew he had to leave in a few days, but he spent as much time as possible with Layla and Tilly. He intended to tell Lord Buckingham about his daughter's condition when he returned home. While she now had her horse, she needed a groom to ride with her, and the grooms hired by her husband were adamant that it wasn't their job. He didn't want to spoil the short time he had here, but it occurred to him that Layla had been imprisoned on this estate since her husband had left in the coach. Jack knew the details of the incident where Layla was compromised because Tilly was a good source of information, although he felt sure she wouldn't share details about her mistress with just anybody. He wondered if it would have been better for her to retire to the country instead of marrying the bounder who was now living with his mistress.

Chapter Eleven

Layla and Tilly were sad to see Jack leave, but now that her horse was in the stable, Layla intended to continue riding. Because the grooms refused to accompany her, Layla was restricted from riding around on the property. While she enjoyed her outings, she was concerned about Max. When he arrived, he was happy and outgoing, but over the last few weeks, Max had become less outgoing and looked unhappy and nervous while caring for Dancer. When Layla ended her ride, she waited as Max helped her from the saddle. As he lifted her down, his sleeves slid up, and the bare arm that Layla could see was covered in bruises.

Once Max turned out Dancer, Layla said," Tell me about the bruises on your arms."

As she spoke, she pushed his sleeve up, and the bruises she could see were from fingers gripping the boy's arms.

"Who did this?"

"Please, Mistress Layla, don't say anything; it will worsen things. They don't want me here in the stable, and they don't want Dancer here either."

"I'll leave this go for the minute, but if it continues, I will fire them."

When Layla returned to the house, the problem with Max's treatment in the stables nagged at her. What could she do? Jack had taken his gun with him, and Layla knew that even if she told the men she was firing them, they would refuse to leave the property. She was powerless to rectify the situation, but couldn't sit around and let the grooms assault Max. Later that night, Layla confided in Tilly, and her maid was as shocked as Layla was. The only suggestion the girls could think of was writing to Lord Geórge, hoping he knew how to contact Beckett. Layla resolved to write the letter the next day and send one of the footmen with the message. There was no way the grooms would deliver the letter, and unless the footmen were accommodating, she was powerless to fix the problem.

After breakfast the following day, Layla headed to the stables. She greeted Dancer and looked around for Max. Layla felt a chill of fear as she walked through the stalls to look for her young groom. Anger and compassion warred inside her chest when she found him curled in a corner. What kind of men would beat a young, defenceless lad? Layla laid her hand on his shoulder, and he cringed.

"Max, it's me. Come with me, and I will have the cook tend to your injuries."

Layal had to stifle her cry of distress when the boy straightened and stood up. Max had a black eye, a split lip and a bloody nose.

"Come with me, Max, but let me turn Dancer out. Bullies who beat children will also attempt to injure my horse. They can't get to her in the paddock so that she will be safe for a while."

Layla told Max to sit at the table as she hunted for the housekeeper when they entered the house through the kitchen. Mrs Hogkin hustled into the kitchen and drew up short when she saw the lad's injuries.

"Who on earth beat you, young Max?"

"They all helped. Mistress Layla, I can't go back there, I'm afraid."

"Mrs Hogkin, when you have doctored Max, can you set up a place for him to sleep? I have an errand to run, but I don't want him outside until I return."

Mrs Hogkin nodded as she went to work on Max's injuries.

Layla walked through the servants' areas and into the hallway.

"Ellis, I need two of your biggest footmen, and if you have a gun, I would appreciate it if I could carry it."

"Goodness, Mistress Layla; what is happening?"

"I need help to saddle my horse, and then I'm going to ride to my in-laws' place. If Sir Beckett is too busy tupping his mistress to give any care for what happens here, then I will take matters into my own hands. Go to the kitchen and see what the animals in the stable have done to young Max, and then tell me I don't need a gun."

When Layla and the footmen entered the stable, she directed them to Dancer's saddle and tack, and they followed her to the field. Dancer was on the far side of the field, and the footmen groaned.

"Do we have to carry this stuff over to where the horse is?"

"Hand me the bridle and rest the saddle over the rail."

Both footmen looked relieved when they disposed of their burdens, but the blond footman said, "If you aren't going to walk to where the horse is, how will you catch it?"

Layla opened the gate and called Dancer's name. When the mare raised her head, Layla called out, " Come on", and at a steady trot, the horse headed towards her mistress. The footman laughed. "Well, don't that beat running around?"

As the men helped Layla to place the saddle on Dancer's back, she said, "One thing you should know. Dancer will not come for you or the bullies in the stable."

The man shrugged. "I wouldn't know what to do with her if she came."

"There is a mounting block over there, so if one of you could help, I'll be on my way."

Layla headed out the front gate and settled Dancer into an easy lope. If Sir George didn't know how to find Beckett, she hoped he might help her with the grooms. Layla seethed as she thought of her husband hiding somewhere with his mistress. The man had forced the marriage and then, amid a barrage of insults and verbal abuse, had abandoned her. When the house came into view, Layla sighed with relief. She hoped Sir George was home and had time to talk with her. The groom, who appeared from nowhere, helped her dismount and headed towards the stable with Dancer. After a brief wait, the butler answered the door, and as Layla tidied her hair and straightened her dress, he watched her with curious eyes.

"I beg your pardon, Lady Fitzwilliam; I didn't hear your carriage."

"That's because I don't have a carriage; I rode. Is Sir George available?"

"Certainly, Maám. Would you like me to send a footman to the stable to offer your groom refreshments in the kitchen?"

"As scandalous as it is, I rode alone. Please announce me to Sir George."

The flustered butler walked along the hallway and announced her after opening the door. Lady Fitzwilliam and Sir George sat on the settee, apparently taking refreshments. Sir George rose and smiled as Layla entered the room.

"Please forgive my intrusion, but it is urgent that I speak to Beckett, and I don't know how to contact him."

Lady Beckett patted the seat next to her.

"Come and sit down and tell us the urgent matter."

Once Layla sat, the words tumbled over themselves as she recounted the events that had led her to ride here today, starting from when Beckett left after his last visit. Lady Fitzwilliam looked horrified, but Sir George bristled with anger.

"I don't believe we can delay a solution to your problems. It doesn't surprise me that he didn't tell you, but Beckett sailed with the *Indian Maiden* three days ago. He couldn't deal with problems with the latest shipment here because the issue arose at the plantation."

"Can you help me sort out the grooms? They are so out of control that I fear they will kill Max or maim my horse."

"Give me a minute to change, and I will accompany you."

Sir George hesitated for a moment, and Layla saw him frown.

"I know Beckett took the carriage to town with him, so how did you get here?"

"I rode, but you have raised another issue I have. I don't give a toss if Beckett's fancy woman needed transport; he took the carriage, and I am virtually a prisoner in the house. While it scandalised your butler that I rode here unaccompanied, I feel certain the ton ladies would cast me out if they discovered I ride around the countryside without a groom. I need transport to visit friends or go shopping, but with Beckett gone, I can't even ask for that."

Lady Fitzwilliam shook her head. "Dear me, Beckett has left things in a mess, hasn't he? George, go and change while Layla and I chat, and after you sort out the grooms, you might be able to solve the problem of the carriage."

When Sir George left the room, Lady Fitzwilliam gave Layla a sympathetic look.

"I know the marriage was Beckett's fault, but it seems you are suffering most. Do you think your parents would support an annulment?".

Layla shook her head. "An annulment is only possible if the couple don't... ah... if the man doesn't bed his wife. But Beckett insisted on bedding me, so an annulment is impossible."

Layla blushed at the topic they were discussing and shuddered at the memory of the bedding she had suffered on her wedding night. Lady Fitzwilliam raised an eyebrow.

"Dare I ask? Your shudder when remembering the bedding suggests you didn't enjoy the experience."

Layla said, "Lady Fitzwilliam, the experience is one I wish never to repeat. Nobody told me that the act between a husband and wife could be unpleasant and painful. I felt violated. Beckett told me he would never bed me again, so there would be no children. I did want children, but if that is how you get with a child, I am glad he has decided to leave me alone."

The conversation halted at George's arrival, but Lady Fitzwilliam knew she had much to tell her husband when he returned. Protocol was satisfied when the marriage occurred, but no one had considered how Layla was faring. Lady Fitzwilliam knew why Beckett was unhappy with marriage to a debutant, but Layla had none of the traits his former betrothed possessed. The thought that her son had been less than kind when bedding his maiden wife made her feel ill. After George helped Layla with her staffing problem, Lady Fitzwilliam would discuss with her husband whether they should reveal Beckett's reason for Layla not wanting to be married to a debutant. And while that might make it easier for Layla to understand her husband's aversion to her, it would not make her life any easier.

54

Chapter Twelve

The drive to the house that was now Layla's home was silent.

Layla felt embarrassed to ask her father-in-law for help, and Sir George felt ashamed of his son's treatment of his lovely wife. When they reached the house, Layla untied Dancer from the rear of the coach and turned her out in the field while Sir George went to the front door. The staff expected his arrival, and Ellis opened the door before Sir George knocked.

"A bad situation, eh, Ellis?"

"Yes, sir, it is shameful. And to think the cads assume there will be no repercussions because Sir Beckett is away is equally disgraceful."

Layla hurried to the front door and escorted her Father-in-law to the kitchen. Max was seated at the table, the blood on his face cleaned, but the bruising and swelling were beginning to colour. Sir George looked closer at the boy, asking, "Are there other bruises covered by your clothes?"

Max nodded. "Yes, sir, my arms and chest are bruised."

"Why on earth didn't you report this abuse to Mistress Layla?"

"The men told me that Sir Beckett hired them, and no petticoat would get rid of them."

Sir George, Layla and two footmen approached the stables. Sir George screwed up his nose.

"Do they ever clean these stalls?"

"No, Father-in-law, they are too busy playing cards, and when I told them to clean up the stench, they laughed."

Layla directed the men to the back room, where the grooms gathered around a table with a deck of cards. The sneer on their faces disappeared when they realised that Layla was not alone and the older man with her was Sir George Fitzwilliam.

"These stables are a disgrace. If you are unable to handle the work, I will assist Mistress Layla in finding replacements. I've seen the boy. Who is responsible for the beatings he took?"

None of the stable hands commented.

"Very well, if nobody will own up, I will dismiss you all. You have one hour to collect your belongings and to present yourselves to the kitchen for your wages."

The men looked stunned and then began talking over each other to lay the blame on the main culprit. Sir George shook his head.

"Reg, it appears that your friends are willing to sacrifice you, but you, other men, be warned. I will not tolerate disrespect towards Lady Fitzwilliam and will return at the end of the week. The stable and stalls will be spotless, and you will also clean the saddles and bridles. Each day, you men will exercise the horses for an hour and then groom them. If the stables aren't up to scratch or one of you lays a finger on the boy, I will dismiss you all."

The men looked shamefaced, but Layla was still wary of them.

"Father-in-law, do you wish to take refreshments?"

"Thank you, Layla. I will remain until this rogue leaves the property, so that refreshments would be welcome."

Once they settled in the parlour, George said, "You mentioned needing a carriage. Where were you thinking of travelling?"

"There is an orphanage on the outskirts of town, and I thought I would offer my assistance somehow. From what I've heard, orphanages struggle to feed their charges, and the staff are so busy that any interactions often centre on the rules that staff wish to enforce. Maybe I can read to the littlies or play games, anything to make their lives more enjoyable."

"That's commendable of you. Can you drive a trap? I have one Lady Fitzwilliam used in her younger days, but it would seat you and Tilly. If

I hitch one of my carriage horses up, you could practise before we use Beckett's horses."

The practice went well, and Layla questioned the stable hands about the suitability of Beckett's horses. The hands assured her that Beckett's preferred mount pulled a carriage, and she and Tilly prepared for their first visit to the orphanage.

When the two arrived at the stable, the handsome bay horse stood in the shafts of the trap, and a groom held his head while Layla and Tilly climbed aboard. The groom stepped away, and the smirk on his face troubled Layla, but the horse's reaction to the cart behind him took all of her attention. What had begun as a lurch turned into a full gallop as the horse bolted for the gate. Chuckles behind her confirmed her fears, but she focused on the frantic horse. No amount of shouting whoa or pulling on the reins slowed the terrified animal, and Layla could see this episode ending badly.

The horse lurched from side to side, and Layla and Tilly hung on grimly. Layla was glad that the road was empty of other vehicles, but as they bolted past Sir George's house, she saw the startled look on her father-in-law's face as he prepared to enter his coach.

"Tilly, we need to get his head around. When I pull on the rein, wrap it around the frame."

Layla let the right rein go and put all her strength into pulling on the left side. Tilly wrapped the rein around the post and grabbed the end, helping Layla pull against the horse's mouth. Slowly, with the aid of the upright, the girls pulled the horse's head around, and with its head against its chest, the hysterical animal could move no further. Layla engaged the break and tied off the end. Tilly bolted from the carriage and raced away from the vehicle, and as Layla attempted to release the horse, she could hear Tilly vomiting. Layla's intentions were good, but she couldn't undo the buckles on the harness because her hands shook violently, and she cursed quietly. She needed to release the horse from the apparatus that caused it so much terror, but her hands would not cooperate. Layla looked into her father-in-law's face when a large hand closed over hers.

"Let me do this, Layla. Go and check on your maid."

Layla's legs barely supported her as she walked towards the crouching figure of her friend. Tears streaked Tilly's face, and her bottom lip shook as she tried to regain control.

"I thought we were going to die."

Layla nodded. "I did, too."

The girls hung onto one another until Sir George approached. Layla felt like swooning, but knew that hysterics now would prove nothing. Layla looked back at the horse, no longer regal and confident but a shell of its former self. Its eyes rolled in its head, and foam and blood gushed from its nostrils. Sweat lathered the horse's entire body, and it shook violently.

"What of the horse?"

Sir George shook his head. "I think that trip has broken his heart; we must destroy him. Explain to me what happened."

As Sir George ushered them towards his coach, Layla relayed the morning's events.

"When we climbed into the trap, the red-headed stable hand smirked, but I couldn't challenge him because the other man let the horse's head go, and the horse jumped forward a few times, and before I could stop him, he was bolting through the gates. The stable hands laughed uproariously, but I was so busy trying to save Tilly and myself that I couldn't focus on them."

Sir George's men had pulled the trap into the field, and Layla watched sadly as a groom walked away with the terrorised horse. She turned to Sir George with a determined look.

"This is my fight, and I will fire those men. Do you have a gun that I might borrow, Father-in-law?"

"You can't shoot them. Do you know how to use a gun?"

"Yes, I know how to use a gun, and they don't know I won't shoot them. I intend to scare them and then send them on their way. Even if they thought Beckett would congratulate them for killing me, did they give any thought to his rage when he discovered we had to destroy his favourite horse?"

When they arrived at the house, Sir George handed Layla the gun, and she said to Tilly, "Ask the footmen to meet me in front of the stables. Tell them to hurry, and if you want to watch the show after the ride they gave us, please come too."

Layla watched Tilly hurry toward the front door, and her anger and fear crashed over her. She was glad of Sir George's support.

"Are you sure you want to do this now? Maybe you should have a restorative rum and a few minutes' rest before you tackle the men?"

"If I go inside, they will assume I am too scared to face them. I must take a stand now, but I would welcome your support."

The faces of the men Layla confronted went from amusement to curiosity.

"That little trick you pulled may have amused you, but you didn't consider the consequences. How happy do you think Sir Beckett will be when he discovers Sir George had the traumatised animal killed? You are too uninformed to consider the consequences of your actions, and since that is the case, I am terminating your employment. You have an hour to collect your things and to present yourselves to the butler for your wages."

The head groom smirked at her and said, "How are you going to make us leave? Sir Beckett hired us, and only he can fire us."

"Is that so?"

Layla drew the gun from her pocket and fired a bullet that pierced the ground next to the belligerent man.

"Oh, gosh, I nearly got you! Never mind, I'm sure my aim will improve with practice. Do you want to stay around to see how many attempts I need before I put a bullet in you and your mates?"

Layla fired the gun again, and the bullet landed between the man's feet, which he had spread belligerently to take a stand against her. When the second bullet landed, the men ran for their lives, collecting their belongings as they fled. In the silence of the stable, Layla thought she heard a chuckle, and the next minute, the footmen clapped, and Tilly and George laughed.

"My dear girl, I thought he would soil himself when the bullet landed between his feet. That was a masterful show of strength, and if those men are ever seen in the area again, I suggest you report them to the magistrate. Attempted murder of a peer ought to have them swinging at the end of a rope."

Layla felt her energy begin to flag as they made their way back to the house. She intended to give Tilly the rest of the day off, and she would hopefully climb into bed to forget this morning's trauma.

Chapter Thirteen

Two weeks after the disaster with the trap, a carriage pulled into the driveway and parked at the front of the house. Not expecting visitors, Layla was curious about the identity of the people in the coach. A confident knock on the door preceded a conversation between two men, and the front door closed. When Ellis entered the room, Layla looked questioningly at him.

"Maám, an acquaintance of yours has arrived to talk with you. I have taken the liberty of asking Tilly to join you as you meet your guest."

Layla rose and followed the butler to the front door, where Tilly waited. Ellis opened the door, and the two women stepped over the threshold; before them was a coach that Layla recognised. The driver gave her a wave, and she trotted down the steps, attempting to appear ladylike, even though she was walking faster than was acceptable for women. A man walked from behind her Father's small coach, and Layla's ladylike behaviour disappeared. She raced towards Jack with a shriek, and he laughed as she lunged towards him. Tilly's face was wreathed in an enormous smile as she hurried to welcome Jack.

"Your Father sent you a present, and he included Fred and me in the package. After your last letter, Miss Layla, your Father decided that you needed protection from foolish cads, and it disappointed him to realise that Sir Beckett was doing such a poor job of defending you."

"We have a few new grooms, and Max is doing a wonderful job, so Fred, if you want to follow the path to the back, the carriage horses can be stabled. Come to the kitchen as soon as you finish."

With the arrival of the carriage, Layla felt buoyant. She and Tilly could now venture away from the house. As none of the society ladies had visited her, Layla decided to put the carriage to better use than calling on women she didn't particularly like. Her priority would be to visit the orphanage and see if she could offer her assistance. It went without saying that Jack and Tilly would join her on her visits, and Layla hoped they could be of use to the orphans. The first visit was to notify her in-laws of her Father's generosity and assure them that while Jack and Tilly would remain with her, her Father was paying their wages.

Layla spent an enjoyable hour with her Mother-in-law, and Lady Fitzwilliam asked Layla to notify her if there was anything she could do to make the orphans' lives easier.

From that day on, Layla, Tilly and Jack became so busy they had no time to socialise. At the orphanage, Tilly worked with the older girls, teaching them how to style a lady's hair, as some aspired to become ladies' maids. Layla read and coloured with the middle group of children, and Jack played games with the boys who had no interest in reading. Layla took a basket filled with the cook's pastries and biscuits to share, and when their visits grew to twice a week, she also brought fruit and vegetables. The visits to the children made Layla sad that she would not have children of her own, but the resilience and good humour of the children always left the three of them smiling.

One afternoon, as they sat in the garden, Jack made a suggestion that seemed so apparent that Layla was surprised no one had thought of helping at the rehabilitation centre when they first discussed their visitations. As a former soldier, the ability to help others was dear to Jack's heart, so Layla tasked him with investigating whether or not she and Tilly would be allowed to help. The matron at the rehabilitation centre welcomed the offer. While Jack played cards with some patients, Tilly wheeled soldiers into the sunshine. Layla found herself serving as a scribe; men with arm and hand injuries, or in one sad case, a man who had lost his sight, wrote letter after letter to send to their loved ones. The soldier who lost sight asked Layla to read the letters from home, and she occasionally read to the men. As they travelled home one day, she said to Tilly, "Who said we were doing a great job helping the orphans and the soldiers? I feel privileged to be involved in their care, and I can't understand why more people don't assist."

Tilly laughed. "You are a woman among millions, my lady. The other society ladies are so busy trying to impress each other and wear more expensive clothes than their counterparts that they don't consider anything but themselves."

The glow of the day dimmed considerably when Sir George arrived unexpectedly. When Ellis showed him in, it was evident that something was amiss. Layla rose to meet her Father-in-law, and he grasped her hands. With shuddering breaths, he said, "The Indian Maiden is lost, and there are no reports of survivors. She went down due to a storm, and everyone on board perished."

Layla gripped Sir George's hand tightly. "Was Beckett on the ship?"

The man nodded sadly. "Yes, he was."

Layla took a shuddering breath and collapsed onto the settee. Beckett was an appalling husband, but she never wanted him dead. Rallying, she opened the door to find Ellis hovering.

"Please, Ellis, Sir George just informed me that Sir Beckett and all hands perished when the Indian Maiden sank. We can forego refreshments, but a good stiff drink may help."

Layla took the decanter and glasses Ellis obtained and poured her Father-in-law a good amount into his glass. As the two sat in silence drinking, a thought came to Layla.

"Oh, dear. How is Lady Fitzwilliam?"

In a choked voice, Sir William said, "The doctor has visited and left a small amount of laudanum. She will sleep for the remainder of the day, but even so, I must go."

"Father-in-law, there is something I need to say. Your family and I know that Beckett and I had far from a good marriage. However, I will not give the biddies of the ton the satisfaction of sniggering about our situation. I will wear morning attire for the year society requires. I will do whatever I can to help. Please call me if you think of some way for me to assist."

After showing Sir George out, Ellis knocked on the door.

"Come in."

"Maám, I am sorry for your loss. Would you like me to call Tilly?"

"Thank you. Yes, please ask her to join me."

The news stunned Layla, but she knew her feeling of disbelief was far from the overwhelming grief her in-laws were suffering. When Tilly arrived, Layla had decided on the best course of action. As Tilly entered, Layla said, "Ellis, will you ask Fred to get the carriage ready? We need to go to town."

Tilly gave Layla a curious look.

"A trip to town is not the usual response to a bereavement."

"Tilly, we both know I had no love for the man, but my in-laws are suffering. A trip to the modiste should secure one black dress for Lady Fitzwilliam and me, and I can order more for delivery later in the week. We need black armbands for the butlers, Sir George, and black wreaths for the doors. I can do that so they don't have to think about it."

"You, my lady, are an exceptional woman. After what you suffered at his hands, it speaks volumes that you would do this for Sir Beckett's parents."

The trip to town proved successful. The modiste had measurements for Layla and Lady Fitzwilliam, and two off-the-rack dresses would suffice until the woman had time to make individual dresses. Laden with the afternoon's haul, Layla asked Fred to stop at the Fitzwilliam's house before continuing to their place. The staff in the house had drawn the blinds, and Layla was uncertain whether or not the butler would answer the door. When the man responded to her knock, he opened the door only enough to say, 'We are in mourning; please go away."

"Grimes, it is Lady Layla. I have some things I think your master might need. Please open the door enough so I can show you what I have."

The butler opened the door, and his eyes glistened when he saw what Layla had in her packages.

"God bless you, Lady Layla. I will give these to Sir George immediately."

On the short trip from the Fitzwilliam's house to Layla's, the girls remained silent until Layla said, "There are people like the butler who are distressed about Beckett's death, so the man must have been civil to some people."

"You're right. It's a pity Sir Beckett never showed you that side of him."

Chapter Fourteen

Layla visited her in-laws the following day with a specific task in mind. When Grimes opened the door, he peered out to see who would call at a house in mourning. Recognising Layla, he opened the door and allowed her entry.

"Please, Grimes, I need to speak with Sir George. The matter is important, and we shouldn't delay it."

The butler said, "Follow me," and proceeded along the hallway. Sir George lifted his head when the butler opened the door, and her Father-in-law's demeanour made her reconsider her visit. His drawn face and slumped shoulders told of his distress at losing his son. Layla gripped her hands and said, "Father-in-law, I'm sorry for intruding, but we must undertake an urgent task."

Sir George waved the butler away after asking the housekeeper to bring refreshments to his study.

"I apologise that Lady Fitzwilliam won't join us; she is still too distraught to talk to anyone."

The conversation ceased as the housekeeper bustled into the room with a tea tray laden with biscuits and pastries. Layla did the tea-pouring ritual, and when she and Sir George held teacups, she worded her conversation carefully.

"This is a delicate subject, and I apologise if you think I overstep the mark, but I need to discuss something with you."

Layla waited for Sir George's nod of agreement before commencing.

" For the entirety of our marriage, Beckett lived in another residence from me, and his mistresses resided there too. I don't believe it would be right if the woman heard about Beckett's death from gossip around the ton. We must inform her, and I would pay her the courtesy of a call, but I don't know where they live. Is there a way to discover the address of his other residence?"

"Goodness, I never gave the woman a thought. Beckett's lawyer must have the information, so if you give me a few minutes, I will write him a message stressing the urgency of a response."

Layla sipped her tea as Sir George scribbled on a piece of paper before sealing it and calling Grimes into the room.'

"Grimes, it is urgent that Franklin Oates receives this and acts on it immediately. Choose a few grooms and send them on their way."

When the door closed, Sir George said, "Are you sure you are the right person to inform your husband's mistress of his death?"

Layla nodded. "If not me, then who? You do not need to further distress yourself; it would be cruel for a footman to arrive with this news. You forget that I am the least distressed person associated with Beckett, and my grieving is not for him but for you and Lady Fitzwilliam. Let me do this for the woman."

"Thank you, Layla; you are not only beautiful on the outside but on the inside as well. Beckett was a fool to reject you without knowing you."

"I have to agree, but he cannot rectify that mistake now. Should I return home and wait for your message to collect the address? I will wear a day dress; if I arrive in mourning clothes, the woman will immediately know why I'm there, and I don't want to deal with a swooning woman."

Two hours later, a messenger from Sir George's home arrived with the news that she could return to her in-laws' house at her earliest convenience. Layla changed her clothes and asked Tilly and Jack to accompany her. When she arrived, it surprised Layla to see another carriage parked in the driveway, and she suspected it might be Beckett's lawyer. Grimes opened the door before Layla could knock and escorted her to the sitting room. A man she didn't know sat in an armchair, and Sir George and Lady Fitzwilliam sat close together on the settee.

Layla bent and kissed her Mother-in-law on the cheek and then sat. Sir George did the introductions, and then the lawyer took the floor.

"Lady Layla, as you are kindly going to inform Miss Desiree of Sir Beckett's demise, I feel it would be sensible for her to know of the arrangements that my client made for her in case of his death."

The pompous man peered at the document and cleared his throat.

"Sir Beckett has left five thousand pounds for Miss Desiree and the house and contents at Ravener Square to do with as she sees fit. The remainder of Sir Beckett's wealth will go to his Father, as will the manor house he owns."

Layla sat still, hoping there was more. Was she selfish to ask the question, "What about me?"

"Sir Beckett left a letter for you, Lady Layla."

Layla gaped. "A letter? So he gets to deliver his last insult from the grave as he has made me homeless and destitute."

The lawyer fiddled uncomfortably before handing Layla the letter and dispensing the address for Layla to visit.

After the lawyer left, Sir George said, "My son is no more, but I am ashamed of his behaviour. Open the letter, dear and see what he has to say."

With trepidation, Layla broke the seal. The letter contained one sheet of paper, and Layla began to read. As she finished the message, she collapsed onto the seat and wept with her face in her hands. Sir George grabbed the letter, and when Lady Fitzwilliam asked him to, he read it out loud.

Mr Dear Unwanted Wife, if you are reading this, you know I am dead and have left you nothing of my estate. I regret not having the pleasure of watching you struggle as you try to manage without servants and my money to bolster your coffers. Spoiled, self-centred, entitled hussies like you deserve nothing. If money is too tight, sell yourself to a doddering old fool and hope he dies before he gets you with a child.
Your unwilling husband, Beckett.

As Sir George finished the letter, Lady Fitzwilliam raised a shaking hand to her throat and said, "What did we do wrong when we raised him? He is a spiteful, angry man, and I feel we have failed in his upbringing."

Sir George looked as shattered as Layla felt, but he said, "Layla, regardless of what Beckett planned, you will remain living in the house, and I will pay your staff from his bank account. My son may have had no morals, but I will not see you homeless or destitute."

"Thank you, Father-in-law. I can't imagine how much harder this marriage would have been without you and Lady Fitzwilliam's support. I must quickly go because I'm sure Miss Desiree will hear of Beckett's death from one of the malicious ladies of the ton unless I beat them to her house."

Lady Fitzwilliam said, "In light of that dreadful letter and the will, are you still committed to meeting this woman who did you out of what rightfully should have belonged to you?"

Layla nodded. "Beckett's mistress didn't cheat me out of what should have been mine; Beckett did that. This debacle is not Miss Desiree's fault, and I still believe she deserves to hear about his death from someone with a little tact and kindness."

Chapter Fifteen

The house at Ravener Square was smaller than the manor house where Layla resided, but it was a stately building with an impressive entryway. Layla asked Tilly to accompany her, and the two women approached the imposing front door. After waiting a few moments, a butler arrived and asked them to state their business.

"I am Lady Fitzwilliam, and I would like to speak to your mistress."

The butler looked disgusted and looked down his nose at the visitors.

"Madam, I don't believe Miss Desiree will want to speak with you."

As the butler went to close the door, Layla slapped her hand against the wood.

"Do you, sir, want your mistress to find out that her lover is dead when some spiteful biddy comes to gloat, or would you prefer me to break the news to her gently?"

The butler's bluster evaporated, and the man's face paled as Layla's imparted news sank in. Without another word, the butler opened the door wide and ushered the women inside.

"Does Miss Desiree have a special servant to sit with her and comfort her when I break the news?"

"Ah, yes, I will call her lady's maid. Give me a moment to send the women to the parlour."

Layla and Tilly sat on the luxurious settee that adorned the room, listening as the women's outraged voices rose. Layla conceded that it was unusual for the wife to call on the mistress, so the agitated voices of the lady of the house and her maid were not unexpected. It suddenly occurred to Layla that she was about to come face-to-face with the woman Beckett preferred to live with rather than his hated wife. When the door burst open and the woman entered, it was apparent why

Beckett spent his time with her; she was beautiful, with long blonde locks and a shapely figure. Without makeup and other adornments, the woman had a clear complexion, and Laya felt a swirl of jealousy strike her; not only did this woman have her husband's high regard, but the inheritance would set her up for life.

"What the devil are you doing here? I will ensure that Beckett is aware of your intrusion into my house. That dratted lawyer was supposed to ensure that you never discovered the address of our home. Beckett said you were an entitled, self-centred hussy, and your presence here only confirms what he has told me. Get out of my house, now."

Layla remained seated, shaking her head.

"Beckett never approved of me, but I am confident he would approve of my visit under the circumstances. Instead of shouting at and insulting me, plenty of which I have suffered from your lover, ask why the wife would visit the mistress."

Miss Desiree settled in a seat and glared at Layla.

"Don't keep me in suspense. What does the despised wife have to say to the beloved mistress?"

Layla grimaced at the woman.

"You know, your attitude tempts me to walk out and leave you to your own devices. I may be the despised wife, and you, the beloved mistress, but I came today because I thought someone with empathy should talk to you. I'm fast reconsidering my actions.'

Layla stood. "Tilly, let's go. Madam, ask your damn butler why I came."

"Stop, stop. You have bad news about Beckett; is that what you came to tell me?"

Layla turned. "I am sorry to inform you that the Indian Maiden has disappeared, feared sunk, with no report of survivors. Beckett was aboard the vessel."

The woman let out a loud wail and sank back against the chair, tears streaming down her face. Her sobs shook the woman, and Layla opened the door to find the butler hovering.

"Find a decanter and a glass of something strong for your mistress."

Minutes later, the butler rushed into the room with a decanter containing a golden-coloured liquor. Pouring a large portion, Layla handed the glass to the distraught woman and urged her to drink. After a healthy swig, the woman composed herself, although the tears didn't stop.

"If you're up to hearing about the arrangements Beckett made for you, I can tell you now, but I'm sure the lawyer will call in a day or two."

Desiree took another gulp of the brandy and shuddered as it hit her stomach.

"I knew he would make some arrangements for me because we discussed the dangers of sea travel, but I never thought it would happen. What did he arrange for me? What did he leave me?"

"Five thousand dollars, this house and all the furnishings and extras. The bequest stated that you could do what you wished with the house, so if you wanted to sell it and move away, that would be your choice."

Layla knew the woman would shed more tears for her worthless husband, but she didn't need to be here to listen to any more grief. When she stood, Beckett's mistress stood too.

"Thank you for coming to tell me. By now, the dowagers of the ton will be gleefully rubbing their hands together, racing each other to pay a condolence call on me. I can have Hannon refuse all visitors, although if you could return to help me with my arrangements, I would be grateful."

Layla thought the request strange but nodded.

"I will call in a day or two."

The trip home was quiet, but Layla hadn't shown Tilly the letter left for her from her husband or mentioned Beckett's will, and she knew she would have to confide in her before word of her newly impoverished state became public. Thoughts of Beckett's cruelty and disdain had receded as Layla dealt with the grief-stricken mistress, but now, with nothing else to distract her, she once again wondered why Beckett hated her so much. With her husband gone to a watery grave, Layla knew he would never be able to answer her questions regarding his hatred of her.

Life for Lyla continued in the same vein, although now she found herself caught up in the arrangements Desiree was putting into place for her future. She confided to Layla that she wanted a husband and a family, but that would not be possible with her reputation in England. Desiree had decided to move to America, where the men hunting for wives outnumbered the available women. Layla thought Desiree's idea was good, but she was concerned about her travelling alone with large sums of money.

"Desiree, do you have a footman that you trust explicitly?"

Desiree stared at her new acquaintance and tapped her chin.

"Yes, I believe I have two or three men who would fit the bill; why?"

"I'm concerned about you travelling alone. Why not ask a footman to accompany you for protection? Once you settle in America, you could pay for his ticket home, or if he wishes to stay, give him a lump sum to set himself up for a new venture. Also, if you spread the money that you are taking over numerous trunks, you are less likely to be robbed."

While Desiree finalised her affairs in England, Tilly and Layla sewed coins into the hems of all her dresses and made money belts for Desiree and the footman to wear underneath their clothes. They unpicked the trunks' lining, secreted notes under the lining, and did the same with the footman's coats. As Tilly and Layla headed home one afternoon, Tilly laughed.

"Who could have imagined that you and I would act as seamstresses for Beckett's mistress? You have none of the money she has for a new life. It doesn't seem fair to me."

Layla shrugged. "We all knew he hated me, but the depths of his hatred only revealed themselves after his death. There is no way to change the past, but I must admit that I'm not sure I'd have managed without Sir George. I don't mind helping Desiree because I have a support group of people, but she has no one. I don't know if Beckett understood her desire for a family or that she would be brave enough to leave the country to obtain what she wants."

"What do you want, Mistress Layla, now that you are a widow?"

Layla shrugged. "You failed to mention an impoverished widow. I'm not looking to marry again; once was enough. Any man who thinks to court me will have to be remarkable. I don't care about titles or wealth; I want a man who genuinely cares for me, if I were to marry again. I will never again marry a man to prevent a scandal or to restore my reputation. You've seen how well that worked out."

Now that Desiree was ready to leave, Layla spent the day with her Mother-in-Law. The two women had always got along well. Still, Lady Fitzwilliam carried guilt for what her son had done to this lovely woman. No amount of soul searching could explain the hateful letter her son penned for Layla, and the thought that without her husband's help, Layla would have to return to her family home and hope for their understanding and support grieved her. The women sat together and chatted as Layla pieced together a new shirt for one of the growing boys at the orphanage.

"Is the mistress ready to sail for America?"

"Yes, I have offered to drive her to the ship tomorrow. Jack and the footman accompanying her can load the trunks, and she will be ready when the ship sails. I admire her courage in going to a foreign country to start a new life."

"It surprised me that you helped her after telling her about Beckett."

"She didn't have anyone else but her servants, and they follow instructions, not give them. There is something I wanted to ask Desiree, but I never had the courage. It's fairly personal, and if I ask you and you don't want to answer, please ignore my question."

"Ask away, dear, although I'm unsure if I can help."

"Desiree is a beautiful woman, but I don't understand why she had no options other than to become a mistress. But that's not what I want to ask. Does the bedding become less painful for the woman, and if it always feels like your insides are being ripped out, why would a woman become a mistress?"

Lady Fitzwilliam looked at Layla with sadness.

"Dear child, if the man you are with is skilled and cares for you, the whole thing can be enjoyable. You once said that the bedding with Beckett was unpleasant, but from what you are saying now, he must have had no concern for your welfare. The more I hear about my son, the more his behaviour disappoints me."

Chapter Sixteen

Eighteen months later

Grimes hurried to answer the door; although the official mourning period had finished, it was unusual for visitors to call this early in the morning. The sight that greeted him made him step back in shock. A bedraggled man with long hair and a bushy beard stood at the door. As Grimes moved to close the door on the intruder, the man spoke, and the usually blank expression on the face of the butler morphed into astonishment. Grimes looked like he had seen a ghost, and in truth, he had. The unkempt man was none other than Sir Beckett Fitzwilliam.

"Well, Grimes, aren't you going to invite me in?" The butler stepped back hurriedly, and Beckett walked into his childhood home for the first time in eighteen months.

"Where are my parents?"

"In the sitting room, my Lord. Do you want me to announce you?"

"No, if you do before they see me, they will have you sent to Bedlam." Beckett followed the carpet runner, which he remembered his mother had bought many years before. He took a large breath at the sitting room door before opening the door and stepping inside. Sir George looked up from the paper he was reading, and the shock and horror at the man before him made him pale, but the cry from Lady Fitzwilliam had him searching the face of the intruder. Before anyone could speak, Lady Fitzwilliam wrapped her arms around the man and cried.

"Oh, my goodness, Beckett, you're alive."

"It seems I am," he said before they both began to cry.

Sir George was still riveted to the spot as he watched his wife hug the man, and when he spoke, George sprang from his chair.

"Is that you, under all that hair?"

"Yes, Father, it's me, Beckett."

It was many minutes before the hugging and crying stopped, and Lady Fitzwilliam said, "What do you want first? Do you want food, a bath, clean clothes, a rest; say the word, and I will have the servants see to it."

"Could we go to the breakfast room and sit at the table while I eat and explain?"

As he ate, Beckett told a story of pirates and captivity. He said that the Indian Maiden was still afloat, and after they had renamed her, she was plying the seas under the pirate's banner. Most of the crew survived, although a few were lost in the initial scuffle when the pirates boarded the vessel. After the pirates overpowered the men, they forced them to work as slaves on their boat. The ship sailed from India to America, trading their property with unscrupulous dealers. Eventually, their captors became careless, and the crew of the Indian Maiden mutinied, taking control of the ship after disposing of the pirate captain and most of his crew. Sir George and Lady Fitzwilliam listened to Beckett's tale with disgust and awe. They found it hard to reconcile the fact that while they mourned, their son was out in the broader world, fighting for his freedom. After recollecting the past eighteen months, Beckett began to flag, and his Mother called Sir George's valet to prepare a bath for her son and to look through cupboards to see if there was clothing that would still fit him.

When Beckett retired, Lady Fitzwilliam couldn't decide whether to laugh or cry. One worry nagged at her joy.

"When do we tell Layla, and what will her reaction be, do you think?"

"She will be at the rehabilitation hospital now, but I will send a message to her to call on us tomorrow. We can do nothing now but enjoy the miracle we have witnessed. We will need to sort out business and personal matters, but with Beckett exhausted, we must wait until tomorrow morning."

Sir George called Grimes and instructed him to speak with the staff, insisting that they keep the news under wraps until he told Layla that her husband was alive. He had the butler choose a discreet groom to deliver the message to Ellis.

Layla arrived home in high spirits. One of the long-term residents received a visit from his mother today, and plans were underway for him to return home. Layla thought she wouldn't be unhappy if the rehabilitation centre were empty and no longer needed for injured soldiers, but that wish seemed optimistic. After she settled in the sitting room with refreshments provided by Mrs Hogkin, Ellis interrupted her contemplation by presenting the message from Sir George. Layla read the letter curiously; her Father-in-law gave no reason for the meeting but urged her to speak to him before entertaining guests.

"Ellis, do you know what is happening?"

"No, my lady, but Sir George did instruct that we accept no visitors in the morning."

Layla laughed. "Given my social interaction with the local nobility, I doubt callers will inundate our home."

Layla felt uneasy as her carriage approached the Fitzwilliams' house. Ellis was unnaturally agitated and pressed Layla to visit her in-laws as soon as she finished breakfast. Tilly accompanied Layla at Ellis's insistence, which felt wrong. Even though Jack always escorted Layla, Tilly rarely went with her to her in-laws' home. Jack squeezed Layla's hand as he assisted the ladies alight from the carriage. '

"Whatever has happened can't possibly be disastrous, or Sir George would have visited you."

Buoyed by that logic, Layla knocked on the door. Her optimism waned as Grimes opened the door with a sympathetic expression.

"Lady Layla, Sir George and Lady Joan asked me to show you to the parlour."

With trepidation, Layla followed the butler along the hallway, and when he opened the door, she stepped into the parlour. Sir George paced in front of the fire, and Lady Fitzwilliam sat perched on an armchair. Sir George stopped his pacing and faced Layla.

"Thank you for being prompt. I have news that has delighted Lady Fitzwilliam and me but will cause you anxiety."

The door opened before Sir George could continue, and Beckett entered the room. Layla's hand flew to her chest, and she slid to the floor without a word. As Sir George yelled for a maid to bring smelling salts, Beckett watched his wife dispassionately. Concerned with what was happening, Tilly followed the maid as she entered the parlour. The sight of Layla on the ground caused a scream of distress, and she knelt next to her mistress. Tilly looked around the room to see what caused Layla's anguish, and her eyes locked on Beckett.

"Holy Mary, Mother of Jesus, did the devil reject you and send you back to torment my Lady further? Grimes, fetch Jack. We need to leave and tend to Miss Layla."

Minutes later, Jack raced into the room. Tilly had propped Layla against her as they sat on the floor. The silence from the Fitzwilliams angered Tilly. When Jack scooped Layla up, he swung around and left without a comment.

Once the family were alone, George slumped into a chair, and Lady Fitzwilliam dabbed at her tears.

"What on earth were you thinking, walking into the room when I hadn't warned her that you were alive?"

Beckett sniggered. "Who could have predicted she'd manage to swoon so convincingly?"

An incredulous expression crossed Sir George's face, and he said, "Tell me what your Mother and I did to raise an unfeeling beast like you. It might be time to forget the things that hussy who jilted you did and look at others with a clear gaze. Your wife has none of the attributes you accuse her of. She is kind, courteous, and thoughtful. Her smile lights up a room, and her wicked sense of humour has given us reason to smile during this troubled time. You explained what happened to you during the last eighteen months, and my heart bleeds for you that you had to endure capture and slavery, but now it is my turn."

Sir George lifted the decanter of rum and poured himself, Lady Fitzwilliam and Beckett a glass. Once he regained his seat, he began to recount the trials Layla had endured because of his refusal to speak to the grooms, who treated Layla with condescension and disrespect. Sir George told of how she had survived and her compassion towards the soldiers and orphans she visited weekly. When he reached the day they heard of Beckett's death, Sir George recounted how Layla had travelled to town to acquire black dresses for herself, Lady Fitzwilliams, armbands for himself, and the butlers and black wreaths for the front doors.

"My wife went into mourning for me? What hypocrisy."

Sir George let out a frustrated groan.

"And had she not, would you be here criticising her for being heartless? Well, let me clear something up for you, Beckett. Layla felt no more sadness at your passing than she did for your crew, but she donned her mourning clothes in respect for your Mother and me. She didn't want to give the dowagers fuel for gossip, so she played the grieving widow in public for a year."

Lady Fitzwilliam took up the narration.

"Layla thought it best if she advised your mistress of your death rather than allow her to hear rumours or to submit her to the false sympathy of the dowagers. After discovering that you had made her homeless and destitute, Layla pushed her despair aside and travelled to inform and console your mistress. As it turned out, Layla and Tilly spent nine days sewing coins into the hems of Miss Desiree's dresses and made money belts for her and the footman who accompanied her on the journey to America."

"Wait, what? Has Desiree left England?"

"Your mistress confided in Layla that she wanted a husband and a family, and she couldn't have either in England, so yes, she has left."

"Why would Layla help Desiree?"

Lady Fitzwilliam regarded her son. "I asked Layla that question, and she said she had a support team, but Desiree had no one. Desiree was all for heading to America by boat, but Layla suggested she would be a target for all the thieves and scoundrels around without protection. Desiree saw the sense of Layla's suggestion and took a footman with her. The man's task once they arrive is to remain with Desiree until she settles, at which time she will pay him for his passage home or, if he prefers, set him up to live a free life in America."

Beckett swigged the contents of his glass and poured another healthy portion. The tales his parents had told about Layla suffering because of his anger and her selflessness, and her compassion for his parents and mistress in the aftermath of the information regarding his supposed death, shamed him. Had his anger towards Cecilia unreasonably influenced his opinion of Layla?

"I think my anger at Cecilia influenced my opinion of all debutantes, but my evasiveness has allowed me to avoid other women of her ilk, so Layla became a target. The forced marriage did not endear her to me, and the thought of being confined for life to a relationship I did not want made me angrier."

Lady Fitzwilliam glared at her son.

"When will you admit that the forced marriage was your fault? Layla told us that when you entered the room, she ordered you to leave, and when you refused, she begged you to leave. Your confidence that other guests would not search for either of you was the reason you compromised her. Admit this is a true account, or call Layla a liar."

Beckett hung his head. "It is what happened, but when the biddies waltzed into the room, I was angry that she was right about my being alone with her. Do you think there is a way to make this right?"

Sir George let out an ungentlemanly snort.

"Layla's response to your presence and her maid's comment suggests you have an uphill battle."

Chapter Seventeen

As Layla's shock at seeing her husband dissipated, anger replaced it. How dare he walk into the room without allowing his parents time to prepare her? She understood that Beckett's parents would be ecstatic at his return, but his return promised more anger, hatred and vile remarks for her.

Over dinner that night, Layla quizzed her friends about their thoughts on the action she should take. They supported her decision to tell her in-laws that Beckett could not live in the house. After all, why disrupt her life when he would buy another residence where he and his new paramour would live? Even though she had decided on her immediate future, Layla spent a restless night dreaming of worst-case scenarios. The following morning, she abandoned the coach for horseback, and she and Jack headed for the Fitzwilliams' home. Once Jack helped her dismount, Layla walked up the stairs to knock on the door. Grimes was there and ready before she could knock, and Layla gave him a grateful smile.

"Grimes, I am here to see Sir George and Lady Fitzwilliam. Could you announce me, please?"

"Certainly, my lady."

Sir George and Lady Fitzwilliam were together in the sitting room, and both smiled when Layla entered.

"I am sorry about what happened yesterday, my dear. Beckett was supposed to wait until we broke the news of his miraculous return, but he ruined our plans with his early arrival and caused you distress."

Layla gave a wan smile at her Father-in-law.

"I am sure he arrived early deliberately to cause me maximum grief. His plan was successful, so he must feel satisfied with my reaction.

But as much as I rejoice in your good fortune, all that Beckett's return for me means more anger, humiliation and unhappiness. Sir George, I know you own the house, but I beg you to tell him he is unwelcome. If Beckett insists on moving into the property, I will throw myself at my Father's mercy and plead for a place to stay. I would be reluctant to leave the area because of the charities I support, but living with your son is untenable. If he moves in, he will unsettle the staff and me and remain a thorn in my side until he buys another residence for himself and his newest mistress."

"Father, I believe I should deal with this problem."

At the sound of Beckett's voice, Layla's face paled, and she clenched her fists.

"I have nothing to say to you, Sir Beckett."

To Layla's dismay, Sir George and Lady Fitzwilliam slid from their chairs as Beckett took the seat opposite her. Her support team had deserted her, and she felt vulnerable and alone. How was she to put her case when Beckett never listened to a word she said?

"It's probably good that you have nothing to say to me because I have much to say. When I met you, I was mourning the loss of the woman I thought was the one I would spend my life with. She was beautiful, shallow and disloyal. On our wedding day, she eloped with an aged noble whose title and wealth far exceeded anything I could obtain. In my anger and grief, I avoided any interaction with debutantes. Cecilia had proven how entitled, self-absorbed and lacking morals she was, and I tarred all other debutantes with her faults."

Beckett rose from his seat, poured a splash of rum in his glass, and offered one to Layla. She sat watching the man she thought she knew as he revealed himself to her. Returning to his seat, he said, "I was at my lowest point when I met you and wanted nothing to do with another debutant. The night I attended the dinner, I discovered the woman I was supposed to court was the one woman in the world I would not. If I had left the room when you ordered me to leave, or even when you begged me to go, I wouldn't have compromised you and forced the wedding, but my ego believed no one would follow me, and there I was mistaken."

"Finally, you take responsibility for the marriage."

Beckett nodded. "Mother and Father related the trials you suffered because of my abandonment. I was not here to listen to your complaints about the groom, and even if I had heard, I was not intent on making your life easier. As a result, the boy, Max, was severely beaten, and the grooms set you and Tilly up to die."

Layla watched the body language as her husband explained his reasons for his neglect and anger; he gripped his fingers, and if she wasn't mistaken, Layla thought the man before her showed remorse.

"I did the most hurtful, callous thing to you in my will and compounded the insult by writing a hateful letter. Father told me that even though I was supposed to be dead, he felt only disappointment and anger at the lack of endowment and the letter I wrote. Yesterday, as I raged about your perfect swoon, Mother and Father took me to task. They argued that it was time to let go of what Cecilia did to me and begin to live. They replayed the things you did for them, and Deiree and convinced me that you are not entitled, self-absorbed and lacking morals. They spoke of your compassion in dealing with them, your year-long mourning period to quell gossip and the help you gave Deiree to make a new life. I am sorry for the harm I caused you, the anger and hurtful comments I made, and for abandoning you. Please, Layla, I beg your forgiveness; I will understand if you feel you can't absolve me of my sins."

Layla was so stunned that she could think of nothing to say in response to her husband's heartfelt apology. Could she forgive him? The anger at her husband swirled around her for so long it was almost a living thing. To discard her feelings after one afternoon's apology was not something she could do, and although he asked for forgiveness, it would be a long time coming.

"Would you like to have some refreshments? I can call Mrs Murray to bring drinks and pastries."

Layla shook her head as she rose.

"I need time to process everything you've told me, so I must go home."

Layla walked to the door.

"Grimes, will you tell Jack I'm ready to leave?"

Sir George and Lady Fitzwilliam entered the room as Layla walked from the front door to wait for the horses. Beckett watched out the window as Jack approached with the horses, and after exchanging a few words, he opened his arms and engulfed Layla. Beckett felt his blood boil as the man turned Layla and tossed her into the saddle. She laughed, and he gave her a mocking bow and mounted his horse.

"What the dickens is that? Are Layla and her supposed bodyguard having an affair?"

Lady Fitzwilliam raised her eyebrows. "And if they were, you wouldn't have cause to complain after you lived in another residence with your mistress, deserting Layla without transport or protection. The answer is no; they are not having an affair. Jack and Tilly are engaged, and Layla told me that Jack is like the big brother she never had. The three visit the orphanages and the rehabilitation home during the week, and if Layla gains comfort from her maid and her bodyguard, who are we to complain?"

Over dinner that night, Layla told Tilly and Jack all that Beckett had said. From Layla's perspective, Beckett had to display his change of heart before she considered his forgiveness. No matter how heartfelt it was, you couldn't wipe out more than a year's worth of hurt and anguish with an apology. It concerned Jack and Tilly that the reason behind the apology wasn't as honest as Beckett stated, but they were willing to see what, if anything, had changed in his behaviour with Layla.

With her anxiety concerning Beckett eased for the time being, Layla continued her visits to the orphanage and the rehabilitation centre. She wished she could do more for the veterans, but couldn't find a way to make their lives easier. The trips to the orphanage were bittersweet for Layla; the knowledge that she would never have children of her own gave the visits a greater significance because the orphans were the only children she would have. If things improved with Beckett, could she ask him to reconsider that decree? Even the thought of being subjected to the pain and humiliation of their only coupling didn't dissuade her from asking her husband to reconsider. Layla struggled with asking Beckett, but the thought of being subjected to ridicule and insults stopped her in her tracks. Would he laugh at her, or would his new attitude carry over into an intimate relationship with her?

Now that things between Layla and Beckett were less volatile, Lady Fitzwilliam asked Layla to join the family for Sunday dinner, which was always a special meal. Conversation at the dinner table often revolved around the business the Father and son ran. Still, sometimes, it veered to Layla's trips to the orphanage and the rehabilitation centre. Layla felt a mix of happiness and trepidation when Lady Fitzwilliam suggested a charity ball to raise money for the causes. Would people attend a ball held at the Fitzwilliam's property if they knew she would be there? Once Lady Fitzwilliams made the suggestion, her enthusiasm increased, and she organised Layla to help with the planning and execution of the event. As Layla was leaving one afternoon, Beckett waylaid her.

"Layla, I envisage a problem with my Mother's charity ball that no one has considered."

Layla looked at the handsome man who was her husband and shrugged. "Please don't keep me in suspense. What problem can you envisage?"

"You played the bereaved widow to stop the ton from gossiping during my parents' time of grief, but now that I am returned and living with my parents, the gossip will be rife among the dowagers and the society ladies."

Layla felt a frisson of fear run through her. Heavens, he couldn't be insinuating that he should live with her, surely?

Beckett watched Layla's face pale and knew she had connected his comment with the necessary adjustment in his living arrangements. Surely they could live together without causing too much upheaval now that hostilities had ceased?

"Ah, are you suggesting that we should live together for propriety's sake?"

"Yes, I am. I will not interfere in the running of the household and will not prevent your visits to the institutions, but I feel it would be better if we gave the ton the image of a happily married couple."

"How long will we need to keep up the pretence? Because when you find another mistress and move to another residence, the façade will crumble. My previous living arrangements made me a recluse, and not once did the stalwarts of society bother to invite me to an event or call for a visit. Why would our living arrangements matter now?"

"I won't promise there won't be another mistress, but I promise I will not live with her. Our living arrangements matter because, previously, they could pretend they didn't know about our separate lives, but with the ball held in my parents' house, it will be evident that we live apart. The ton is good at pretending they are unaware of societal events, but must comment when it's pushed in their faces. Gossip surrounding our living arrangements might derail the charity ball. Are you prepared to take the blame for the ball's failure?"

Layla looked ill but said, "Please allow me to inform the staff and to give the maids time to air your room. Perhaps after breakfast, tomorrow would suit us."

Beckett bowed to her arrangements and left her in the entry hall, wondering if she would survive this plan.

Chapter Eighteen

Layla shared the news that Beckett would be moving into the house the next day with Ellis, trusting that he would share the information with the staff. She asked Mrs Hogkin to send a maid to Beckett's room to freshen the bedding and dust the room so anyone who hadn't heard the news from Ellis became aware of the imminent arrival of the man who could turn a happy home into a war zone. As Layla ate breakfast the following day, she had to force herself to eat, not wanting to let the staff know how worried she was about her husband sharing the same house with her.

Today was one of the few days of the week that Layla didn't visit local charities and institutions, so without the ability to flee, she forced herself to sit in the sitting room, mending the mountain of clothes from the orphans and the men in the rehabilitation unit. She remained seated when she heard the crunch of carriage wheels on the driveway. If this were to be Beckett's home, Layla did not intend to greet him every time he arrived home. She listened to the footmen carrying trunks and Beckett's deep voice giving instructions, and then the activity caused by Beckett's arrival died away. A conversation ensued outside the sitting room door, and when the door opened, Beckett entered.

"Are you settled into your room? Was everything satisfactory?"

"Yes, thank you. I asked Ellis for some light refreshments because my Mother asked me to discuss details about the ball."

A knock on the door interrupted the conversation, and when the maid left, Layla poured the tea before settling into her chair to discuss the charity ball. Beckett went through a mental list of questions Lady Fitzwilliam wanted answered, and the last question floored Layla.

"Do you have a dress for the ball?"

Layla blinked, processing what Beckett had asked.

Beckett continued. "I know you bought black dresses for your mourning period, but Mother says that she doesn't think you have visited the dressmaker since you have lived here. It would be shabby if you arrived in a dated or worn dress. Can I leave that to you and Tilly to take care of?"

"Um, yes, we will visit the dressmaker tomorrow and order a dress."

"Layla, I may have given away half of my wealth to Desiree, but I am not destitute yet. Please buy more than one dress. After the ball, you may have invitations and must dress appropriately."

Layla snorted. "I'm glad you're not broke because I am."

Beckett looked uncomfortable and said, "You have every right to be angry, but can we put that aside and reside together without anger and barbs? As a rule, women rely on their husbands to support them, and it will be the same with us."

After the initial flurry of activity caused by Beckett's arrival, the house settled into its normal rhythm. As the ball approached, Layla looked forward to it with anticipation. Lady Fitzwilliam had left nothing to chance, and Layla felt confident everything would go to plan. The dress she bought for the evening was a change from anything she had owned before. No longer a widow or a debutant, she could choose brighter colours and more revealing outfits. Her emerald green dress hugged her torso before falling to the floor in a froth of ruffles. The modiste had cut the bodice daringly, revealing some of her cleavage, and as Layla dressed, she wondered if her husband would even comment on her dress.

When she descended the stairs, Beckett stared at his wife as if he had never seen the woman before. He smiled and complimented her on her appearance, but silently cursed himself for not realising how lovely she was.

Lady Fitzwilliam insisted that Layla and Beckett join her and Sir George on the receiving line, so with a smile pasted on her face, Layla suffered the scrutiny and backhanded barbs of the women of the ton. After one too many men had ogled her, Layla scooted close to Beckett, intent on reminding these men that she was married. Beckett placed her hand on his arm without comment, giving her more support. Layla gave him a grateful smile before turning to the next couple. She felt Beckett stiffen, but it wasn't until the woman opened her mouth that Layla understood his trepidation.

"Well, isn't this nice? I applaud your style, Sir Beckett. Once the mistress has fled to America, you crawl back into your wife's bed. I wonder how long she will satisfy you before you look elsewhere?"

Layla glared at the newcomer.

"Madam, you are out of order. I don't know who you are, but this is a charity event; if you wish to argue with my husband, you must wait for a more appropriate time."

The woman chuckled. "Has darling Beckett not told you of his true love, Cecilia?"

Layla felt Beckett tighten his hand on her arm, but she would not let this shrew ruin their evening. Layla laughed at the woman.

"Yes, he did. How pleased I was when I heard you had jilted him because it meant he was free to marry me, although I am sure it is bad ton to elope with another man on your wedding day. The amusing thing about your non-wedding was that Beckett wanted to end your agreement, but he knew that if he did, the ton would consider you ruined. How amusing! You managed to ruin yourself unaided. But never mind, he and his guests enjoyed the refreshments your parents paid for and Beckett and I are happy with the outcome. You've made a spectacle of yourself again, so now I will ask you to leave."

"Grimes, will you ask the footmen to escort this guest from the house? I'm sure we don't need her kind at a charity event."

Layla watched as Grime's ordinarily stoic expression showed a hint of both amusement and surprise before he replaced his unflinching expression. With the efficiency she expected of him, Grimes motioned the footmen forward, and they escorted the woman and her partner from the room. As the woman left, Layla turned to the waiting guest, and seeing their mixed expressions, she said, "Well, that gets rid of the trash." She heard a chuckle from her Father-in-law, and the music resumed, and people began to enjoy the evening or gossip about the argument. Despite the unorthodox beginning, the ball was a huge success, and Layla and Lady Fitzwilliam were happy with the money raised for the two charities.

Beckett stood in the doorway to their adjoining rooms as he removed his cravat. His presence startled Layla, but she nodded when he said, "I will leave you to retire, but thank you for what you said to Cecilia tonight. I never saw the mean side of her until we became betrothed, and then it was too late to undo."

"You're welcome. After her comments, I couldn't have that woman in the house because I may have provided material for the gossipers, but she would have lied to make us look bad. And as we know, the ton doesn't care if what they hear is untrue; the more lurid it is, the better they like it."

As Layla spoke, Beckett continued to undress; by now, he wore only his shirt and breeches, and she found it hard to tear her gaze away from his broad chest. When she finally looked up, he winked at her, and as her face flamed a bright red, he turned and entered his bedroom. Layla's fingers trembled as she braided her hair. Why did she suddenly notice that her husband was a handsome man? The sight of his bare chest mesmerised her, and his cocky wink said that he knew his nakedness enthralled her. How could she face him in the morning? Now that the charity ball was over, would Beckett return to his parents' home, or would he remain in her house?

Layla tossed and turned all night, and when Tilly arrived the following day to help her dress, she was far from refreshed.

"Goodness, miss, you look like you've had a rough night. Was there anything particular that kept you awake?"

"Beckett came into my room to thank me for supporting him at the ball and evicting his former fiancée. But as he talked, he continued to undress until he wore only his breeches and his shirt, undone to his waist. I didn't know where to look, and I wondered when I stopped hating him and began seeing him as a man. He's been different since he apologised and moved here, but is it a facade, or is this behaviour the real person without the anger?"

Tilly watched her mistress, a concerned expression crossing her face.

"You worry that you will become fond of him, only to find that he isn't the gentleman he is now. I don't know what to tell you except that he must have some redeeming qualities for Desiree to tolerate him for so long, and when everyone thought he drowned, people came forward in their droves to express their sympathy. Maybe what you saw at the beginning was not him but his anger at the situation, and now he has resolved his rage; what you see is the nice man everyone seems to think he is."

When Layla arrived for breakfast, Beckett was reading the newspaper. His smile was genuine, and the smirk Layla feared was not present. It seemed that Beckett had forgotten last night's incident, and Layla had no desire to remind him of her ogling his half-dressed body.

Chapter Nineteen

It surprised Layla when Beckett asked to accompany her to the orphanage. She was unsure of his reasons for the trip, but shrugged off the idea that he was checking how the administrators spent the money from the charity ball. There were many things the children needed beyond a bed and meals, and any donated money quickly disappeared as new clothes replaced old or outgrown garments, and books for tuition required upgrading. It was rare for the smaller children to receive new clothes because there were always hand-me-downs from the older children. Layla and Tilly spent hours repairing garments and sewing new clothes, and the need kept them busy. Layla wished she could afford new clothes for the little ones, but she did the best with what she had.

The trip to the orphanage was pleasant, with Beckett making conversation and small talk as they travelled. When the carriage stopped, Jack jumped from the box to help the ladies descend. They made their way to the office, and Layla introduced Beckett to the matron before the group moved into the large playroom. It stunned Beckett when the children swarmed around Layla, Tilly and Jack, but the recipients of the children's welcome laughed. This reception appeared to be a standard response, and Beckett understood the group's critical role in keeping the children's spirits high. Beckett wondered what he could do as the groups broke up to go to activities with the adults. Eventually, Jack called out, "Sir Beckett, do you want to play football with us?"

Like the little children, Layla was missing in the large room when the men and boys returned for indoor games. Beckett looked around, and a flirty assistant sidled up to him. The girl fluttered her eyelashes at him and smiled coyly.

"Hello, my Lord. Since this is your first visit, I'd gladly show you around."

"That's very kind, but I'm looking for my wife. Where have she and the smaller children gone?"

The girl gave a disgruntled look and directed him to a bedroom. Two babies lay sleeping in their cots, but Layla sat on a rocking chair with two little girls snuggled against her, asleep. She looked up when he entered and smiled, and remembering his decree that he would not father any children with her made him ashamed. This woman, his wife, was made to be a mother, and he had denied her that choice for selfish reasons. Layla beckoned him, and when he reached her, she said, "Take Sadie from me and lay her in her bed. I will put Penny in her bed."

Beckett didn't know how to handle this small body, but did his best not to wake his small charge. As Layla lay Penny in her bed, the little girl looked up and said, " Mama?"

"Sh, sweetheart, go to sleep."

The little girl rolled over and closed her eyes, and Beckett thought his heart would break. He decided to investigate the situation of each child abandoned at this facility. Surely there must be families well-placed to give these children a home?

That night, as dinner concluded, Beckett asked Eliis to make sure someone lit the fire in the library and requested Mrs Hogkin to serve their tea there. Layla did not comment when they went to the library, but was curious about what Beckett wanted to do. She had noticed how quiet he was after they visited the orphanage, but he had said little about the trip. When they arrived in the library, the fire blazed brightly, and Mrs Hogkin laid out the teapot and cups. Layla watched her pensive husband and placed his teacup on the small table before him.

"You are quiet tonight, Beckett. What is filling your thoughts?"

"Why do you go to the orphanage?"

"I go because I can make a difference in the sad lives those children live, and I go because if you and I are never to have children, I will pretend those sweet little girls are mine and help them grow into good women."

"What would you say if I suggested we have children?"

Beckett watched with dismay as Layla's face went pale, and she gripped her hands together to stop them from shaking.

"Beckett, I want children, but if you have to violate me like you did the last time, then I will pass. I had never before experienced so much pain; it felt like I was being ripped apart from the inside. When you finished and walked away, I wanted to clean myself, but I didn't think I could walk to the basin, even if I could find it in the pitch black. Eventually, I cleaned myself with the sheet and curled up, hoping to stop the pain. That night was the worst experience of my life, and if I can't have children, it will sadden me, but I won't let you do that to me again."

Beckett slumped in his chair and placed his head in his hands. Layla watched with curiosity. Why did he look so dejected? She had only agreed with his decision on the night of their wedding. When Beckett looked up, Layla could see the shame on his face and wondered why he looked ashamed.

"Dear God, Layla, it seems all I do is apologise for my actions. Bedding a woman can be pleasant for a woman..."

Layla's unladylike snort interrupted Beckett's dialogue.

He shook his head and sighed.

"The night I consummated our marriage, I was furious that you had trapped me into marriage."

He held his hand up to stop Layla's protest.

"I know the fault was mine, but I was angry enough not to think clearly. I took you with anger and force. I was neither kind nor compassionate, and for me to take a maiden so roughly and with no care is inexcusable. When I returned to my room, I felt both guilt and a sense of justification. I felt guilty because I knew I had hurt you, but I felt justified because it proved how abhorrent the marriage was to me. Even though my parents continued to sing your praises, it wasn't until I returned from captivity that I realised they were right. Cecilia had messed with my mind so badly that I couldn't see past my humiliation and anger. Layla, I can make it enjoyable for you. If we go slowly, you can tell me to stop anything you don't like me doing, and I will."

"What will you do first?"

"Lots of kissing is a good start."

Layla looked anxious as she said. " I've never been kissed. I don't know what to do."

"Let's take this discussion to the bedroom, and we'll go from there."

Layla stood in the middle of the bedroom, wondering what came next. She watched as Beckett removed his coat, cravat, and vest, and pulled off his Hessian boots. As Beckett approached, Layla tensed, but when he gently laid his hand on her cheek, she relaxed. The caress was warm and comforting, and when he tilted her head, Layla followed his lead as he leaned in and kissed her. Beckett's lips moulded with hers, and she sighed at the sensation. When the kiss deepened, and Beckett ran his tongue along the seam in her closed mouth, she opened for him. Layla's heartbeat raced as he took control of the kiss, and she barely registered that he had moved her towards the bed. She tensed as her legs hit the bed, but he soothed her with more kisses and quiet words.

Layla followed Beckett's lead and lowered herself onto the bed, and her anxiety at what was to come returned. Much to her surprise, what happened next was more kissing, although Beckett had moved his attention from her mouth to her neck and the swells of her breasts. The feeling was exquisite, and Layla moaned her appreciation, encouraging Beckett to slide her chemise from her shoulders and lavish his attention on her breasts. Beckett returned to lavish his kisses on her face, and with their faces close together, she could see the raw desire on his face.

"Are you all right?"

Layla nodded. "Yes."

Beckett slid her chemise off, and she lay bare beneath him.

"You are so beautiful, Layla. I promise to make this good for you."

Despite her fear of what he was about to do, Beckett continued kissing her and toying with her breasts. When she squirmed beneath him, he ran his hand along her torso and down her legs. He placed his hand on her mound and slid his fingers along the wet folds before circling her clit with his wet fingers. Layla writhed beneath him, mindless to his actions, as he fingered and rubbed her clit. A feeling she had never experienced built inside her, and she opened her eyes wide as the sensation increased. When the wave crashed over her, she slammed her eyes closed and screamed Beckett's name.

As Layla lay on the bed, she felt his intrusion but didn't have the energy to protest. Much to her surprise, this time, she felt full, but the sensation wasn't unpleasant. When Beckett began to move, the feeling started to build again, and Layla pushed herself against him as he increased his speed. Wanting to be as close to Beckett as possible, she wrapped her legs around his hips and squeezed him close. He grunted his release, and the feeling of his seed spilling inside her made her muscles clench and sent the wave crashing over her again.

Beckett pulled Layla against him. His lazy smile made her smile in return.

"You can do that anytime you want, my lord. Now I understand why women become mistresses if they can't have a husband."

Beckett laughed and shook his head.

"There wouldn't be so many mistresses if the ladies of the ton didn't tell debutantes to close their eyes, open their legs and pray that their husband is fast."

"How often do we do this before I am with child?"

"Sometimes it takes months."

Layla smiled and said, "Oh, what a pity. I suppose we will have to do this often?"

Beckett gave a wolfish grin. "As often as we want, my dear, and how I feel now, I will want you lots."

Layla gave a contented sigh and snuggled closer to Beckett.

The budding relationship between Layla and Beckett was evident to everyone who came into contact with the pair. Layla wore a contented expression, and Beckett was more patient and less restless. While Tilly was pleased that Layla and Beckett had finally ended their feud and found comfort in each other, she feared this might be the lull before the storm. Jack told her to enjoy the peace while it lasted, but he shared her concerns. Did a leopard change its spots overnight? He wasn't sure, but he'd enjoy the peace for now.

Chapter Twenty

Layla entered the study, only to find Beckett pacing, a document in his hand.

"Not good news?" Layla queried.

"The worst. There is a delay with the shipment because the natives want a cut of the profits. I pay my workers well; they have free housing, but giving them part of the profits will not happen. Our company covers the costs of planted seedlings and stock, as well as any necessary soil modifications. So, why should the natives receive only half the profit? If I closed my operation, they would end up in poverty because none of them have the seed money to continue the business, and none possess the necessary business acumen. If I sail the Indian Maiden away from their shores, who will carry the stock?"

"Please tell me you aren't returning there after what happened last time you sailed?"

Beckett wrapped his arms around Layla. "I fear I must return, or our holding there will be lost."

Layla buried her head in his chest, listening to the heartbeat she would miss in the night once he left. How was it possible to finally find happiness together, only to have world events rip them apart?

"When will you leave?"

"I'll discuss it with my Father, but it needs to be soon, or there will be nothing to save. If the natives get it in their heads to make us pay, they could be illogical enough to torch the fields, not thinking they're destroying their livelihood. All it needs is a few rabble-rousers, and the situation could get out of control."

Layla knew Beckett travelled more often than Sir George, who blamed old age for his more sedentary lifestyle, but the thought of him sailing to India panicked her. The last time pirates attacked the ship, he was missing for eighteen months. When he was presumed dead, the news only affected Layla because she had to support her in-laws. If Beckett were lost at sea again, she would have to deal with her grief. Layla had never told Beckett that she loved him because she wasn't sure he felt the same; however, she would tell him tonight, with time running out. They had to curtail their planned evening together because Beckett wanted to leave at daybreak. As Layla lay in Beckett's arms, she said

"I must tell you something you mightn't want to hear."

She could hear the grin in his voice when he said, "Alright, spit out your unwanted information."

Layla propped herself on her elbow and looked into his eyes.

"Beckett, I love you."

Silence greeted her; he flipped her until she lay on her back. He ran the back of his knuckles along her cheeks and said, "It took you long enough. I've wanted to hear that ever since the second time I tupped you. I can't believe I fell in love with the argumentative wench who wrangled me into marriage, but I did. I love you too, and I'm damn glad you said it tonight because I'd hate not to have heard it if something happened to me."

Fear seized Layla, and she could barely speak. After a moment, she said, "Promise me you will return."

Beckett grasped her hand in his, entwining their fingers. "I promise I'll do my best."

Three months passed before Layla was sure she was with child. She desperately wanted to tell Beckett, but his ship wouldn't return for another month or two. All those around her worked on the theory that no news was good news, but Layla thought the ominous silence was a concern. What was happening on the other side of the world that was taking so long? Even though Beckett had taken steps to make the ship safer, Layla couldn't dispel the feeling of dread that filled her. Lifeboats and mounted guns could deal with most things at sea, but the real danger, when Beckett discussed the issue, was the native workers. Everyone told Layla she needed to relax because her focus should now be on the babe she was growing, but she couldn't get the danger Beckett faced out of her mind. Once he returned, she would insist his trips across the sea ended.

While Beckett was away, life continued much as it had with visits to the orphanage and the rehabilitation centre. Laya wondered how much longer she could make the trips because society's laws prohibited pregnant women from being out and about. It seemed that the society people subscribed to the idea that babies were found under cabbages and didn't want the evidence to disprove this theory on the streets. Now that the doctor had confirmed her pregnancy, Layla spent time sewing clothes for her newborn baby and repairing clothes for the orphans. Not having come into contact with many new babies, Layla relied on her mother-in-law to advise her on what she needed. Sir George and Lady Fitzwilliam were excited to be grandparents, and Laya felt confident that both sets of grandparents would spoil the baby. Time passed, and Layla heard nothing about when the Indian Maiden would arrive. Layla was so frustrated that she vowed to Tilly that if she didn't soon have news of the ship's arrival, she would travel to the docks to discover what was happening. What stopped her from travelling anywhere was the whispered comment from one maid to another about Beckett hiding in his parents' house. The statement floored Layla, and although she decided it was a vicious rumour, she asked Tilly to question the maid. When Tilly returned from her conversation, Layla discovered the tale was accurate. Her husband had returned and had moved in with his parents. Beckett's promise to return and declaration of love were worthless words spoken at the height of passion.

By now, Layla was close to six months gone with the babe and her increased bulk made travelling uncomfortable. With regret, she had cancelled her visits to the orphanage and the rehabilitation centre. Still, Jack and Tilly continued the trips and often came home with drawings from the children or well-wishes from the soldiers. Sitting at home, waiting for news of Beckett, had been an endless waste of time and energy, especially if he was staying at his parents' house. With her anger roused, Layla decided to confront her husband and in-laws to ask for an explanation. She asked Jack to tell the driver to bring the carriage around, and she would take Tilly for support.

Layla levered herself from the carriage with Jack's assistance when the carriage stopped at the front door of the Fitzwilliams' home. Grimes opened the door when she knocked, but he looked nervous, a feat for one of the most stoic butlers she knew.

"Good afternoon, Grimes. I would like to see my husband. Would you tell Sir Beckett I am here?"

"Ah, ma'am, follow me, and I will allow Lady Fitzwilliam to explain."

"Explain what?"

"Please, Mistress Layla, follow me."

Completely confused and furious, Layla waddled after the butler. When she entered the sitting room, her in-laws were in attendance, but her husband was absent.

"Dear, please, take a seat."

Layla remained standing. "What did I do to have Beckett move into your house instead of mine? Why did I have to hear that my husband had returned from the maids whispering to one another? Why would you keep the news of Beckett's arrival from me? You knew how worried I was, yet you kept the word of his arrival to yourselves? I'm angry and hurt. Where is he? I intend to give him a piece of my mind." Layla sat suddenly, her anger dissipated by the grief overtaking her.

"He told me he loved me. He promised he'd return. Why would he do this to me?"

Sir George rose and handed Layla a nip of brandy. She shuddered as the fiery liquid hit her stomach.

"Layla, I tried to convince Beckett to let me notify you of his arrival, but he refused. There was an uprising at the plantation, and Beckett received severe injuries. He has regained his health, but has terrible scars he doesn't want anyone to see. He says he looks like a monster and refuses to see you."

Layla processed what her Father-in-law had to say and then cocked her head in inquiry.

"How do you know he has terrible scars if you haven't seen them?"

Lady Fitzwilliam sighed. "We have seen the scars, and I agree with Beckett that they are disfiguring."

"So he thinks it is fitting that his parent should see him but not his wife? Where is he? I want to talk to him."

"He is in his room but won't let you in."

"We'll see about that."

Layla heaved herself from the armchair and waddled towards Beckett's bedroom. After the stress he put her through by returning to the plantation, Layla was not ready to allow the man to hide from her. As she arrived at Beckett's bedroom, she tried the doorknob, and when it turned in her hand, she pushed the door open and entered. Beckett stood with his back to her, thinking his Father had entered the room, and said, "Has she left?"

"No, she hasn't."

Beckett hunched his shoulders and stepped further away from his wife. "I have nothing to say to you, madame. You are invading my privacy, and you must leave."

"Well, dear husband, I have plenty to say to you. When you left, you promised you would return if you could; you told me you loved me, and this is how you treat the woman you purported to love? I haven't seen the damage to your face, so I can't sympathise with you, but do you believe I will be so disgusted that I will swoon and cause a fuss? Before you left, we spent months together, and I miss you. Please come home. Our baby will be born in a few months, and he or she will need a Father, and I need my husband."

Beckett growled. " Don't fool yourself, wife. I only bedded you because I couldn't afford to house a mistress. Your inexperience in the bedroom and clumsy attempts to seduce me were not enough to keep me interested. The things I told you were to keep you in my bed while I had no alternative. If things had gone differently, I would have returned with one of the young, nubile women who kept me satisfied while I was away, and if you think I want to tup you now that you are as big as a whale, you must be delusional. Get out, Layla. I don't want you; I never did."

Beckett strained to hear what Layla was doing and cursed aloud when he overheard her sobs. How long would it take her to realise he had done her a favour? Living with a monster, which was what Beckett had become, was no life for a beautiful young woman. He hoped that by being unkind and, for the most part, untruthful, the nasty comments would reignite Layla's hatred of him.

Chapter Twenty-One

Tilly mopped Layla's forehead as she strained to bring her baby into the world. Over the last months, her contact with the Fitzwilliams had decreased because she found carriage rides too uncomfortable. Besides, why torture herself with proximity to her husband if he would not talk to her? Another pain ran across Layla's belly, and she groaned with the intensity of the wave. The midwife encouraged her, and Tilly supported her with kind words and loving touches. Layla knew that Jack was pacing outside the door, anxious for her, so she kept her moans and shrieks subdued. She was ready to give up this fruitless exercise when the midwife said, "One more push, my lady and your baby will be here." Layla cried when the midwife handed her the shrieking, red-faced infant, and she immediately fell in love. A cheer came from the other side of the door, and Layla realised that Tilly had conveyed the news of the little boy's arrival to the men waiting anxiously.

A convoy of visitors arrived randomly after the birth of little Matthew. Maggie and Theo were the first visitors, and Layla was thrilled to see her sister. Maggie stayed for two weeks to help settle her sister and little nephew, and when she left, Layla promised to visit once she had time. After her sister departed, Layla's parents arrived, and while Lady Buckingham was more a hindrance than a help, Layla gritted her teeth and thanked her Mother for her advice. Layla had no intention of following most of the advice, but it cost nothing to be polite. The one person who didn't visit was her husband, and Layla knew that Jack had contacted her in-laws shortly after the baby was born. A message from her in-laws assured her they would see Layla and the baby after her family left, and true to their word, they arrived three days after her parents' departure.

When the carriage arrived, Layla waited anxiously to see if Beckett had accompanied his parents, and her disappointment was hard to hide when it became clear that he was not with them. Lady Fitzwilliam and Sir George fussed over Matty and proclaimed him the most perfect grandchild a couple could have. Despite wanting to know what Beckett was doing, Layla refused to ask, and neither her husband nor her in-laws offered any information regarding his well-being. A wave of despair washed over Layla as her visitors departed, and she wondered if she was to remain in limbo for the rest of her life. Layla was no longer a single woman but was neither a wife nor a widow. How long could she stay here, close to her husband but far away?

That night, over dinner, Layla dismissed the servants and asked Ellis to close the door on his departure.

"You know, as does most of the staff, that Beckett refuses to see me. The one time I saw him since his return, he said awful, hurtful things and mocked my inexperience in the bedroom. I thought we connected, but he said he couldn't afford a mistress when he returned and decided I may as well earn my keep."

Jack made a savage sound, and Layla felt sure that Jack would attack him if Beckett were in the house. Tilly took Layla's hand and squeezed gently.

"My situation is untenable. I am neither a single woman, a widow, nor a wife. I may have to wait years for Beckett to acknowledge me, but after his treatment, when he told me he loved me, I could never trust him again. My options are limited, but I think divorce might free me."

Jack shook his head. "The justices rarely grant a Lady a divorce, and the damage to your reputation would be catastrophic."

"So you suggest I sit here, abandoned by my husband and become an old maid?"

Jack grimaced and ran a hand through his hair.

"Would your Father support your application?"

Layla nodded at Tilly.

"Yes, I do believe he will. He feels guilty about insisting I marry Beckett, and he came to my aid when I had trouble with the grooms."

"If the justices grant you a divorce, what would you do then?"

"Maggie and Theo have offered to house me, and they are happy for you two to join me, although if you want to return to my Father's estate, I would understand. I guess there is no time like the present, so tomorrow, I will see my in-laws, and they can convey the news to their reclusive son."

That night, Layla lay in bed and wept. Her marriage, which started as a hateful agreement and morphed into a loving relationship, was completely dead. While the things Beckett said about Layla's ineptitude in bed were hurtful, Layla guessed they were his way of pushing her away. So, if he wanted to remove her from his life, she would agree to his wishes, except she would end this farce of a marriage. The carriage stopped at the front door to the Fitzwilliams' home, and Jack jumped down from the box to help Layla exit the vehicle. He squeezed her hand in support and then rapped on the door. Grimes opened the door so quickly that Layla was sure he had heard the carriage approach, but she merely inclined her head and said, "I would like to see Lady Fitzwilliam and Sir George."

"Lady Fitzwilliam is in the parlour, and I will call Sir George from his study."

"Grimes, is Lady Fitzwilliam alone?"

"Yes, maám, she is alone."

Layla walked towards the parlour as Grimes left to call Sir George. Lady Fitzwilliam looked surprised at the unexpected visitor but smiled and stood to hug Layla.

"You didn't bring Matty with you?"

"No, I have a serious matter to discuss with you and didn't want him to waylay the conversation."

Sir George entered before his wife could ask more questions, and Layla smiled at her Father-in-law.

"Where is my grandson?"

Layla laughed. "Your good wife has already queried me about his absence, but I have something important to discuss, and when Matty is present, the conversation revolves around him."

Lady Fitzwilliam, the consummate hostess, said, "Do you want refreshments, dear?"

"Maybe later, if you don't mind."

Layla clenched her hands in her lap.

"I have been married to Beckett for three years, more or less. During that time, he spent most of his life at sea or with other women and mistresses. The marriage was supposed to save my reputation, but Beckett spent his time blaming me for something that was entirely his fault, and he has spent most of our acquaintance punishing me for imaginary slights. Instead of restoring my reputation, he made me the comic relief for the ton. After Beckett returned from the dead, he seemed to accept the responsibility for our plight, and we lived together in harmony. Before he left, he told me he loved me and promised to return. Imagine my distress after fretting about his late return when I discovered he came here instead of honouring his promise. He will see his parents but not his wife. The one time I talked to him, he made foul and hurtful comments that I find hard to forgive. Refusing to see or even acknowledge his son is the final straw. I am done with Beckett and intend to apply for a divorce. I am confident that my Father will support the application."

Lady Fitzwilliam gasped. "Dear, do you have to divorce Beckett? Couldn't you live independently without going to that extent?"

"Mother-in-law, that is what I have been doing, but I refuse to stay in limbo while Beckett hides in his room. I want a husband who cares for me, not someone who belittles me and says hurtful things just because he can. I may never marry again; this first experience leaves a lot to be desired. Any man I marry doesn't have to be a member of the nobility; I will marry a gardener if he respects and honours me, and I care for him. I'm sorry, Sir George, Lady Fitzwilliam, but I must free myself of Beckett's control for my sanity."

Sir George nodded.

"I understand, my dear. Where will you go? I assume you will not want to live in a house a few miles away from Beckett."

"Maggie and Theo have offered me a home. They have an unoccupied dower house, which provides me with a place to live without crowding them. I have offered to take Tilly and Jack with me, but I have also allowed them to return to my Father's estate if they wish."

Lady Fitzwilliam rose. "I need a rest; your news, Layla, is disturbing. Have you asked your Father for his assistance?"

"No, that is my next job."

Lady Fitzwilliam kissed Layla on the cheek and left the room. An awkward silence settled over the room, and Layla rose, intending to make her escape. Sir George escorted her to the door and patted her shoulder.

"I regret that it has come to this, but I understand you want more from life than my son will offer. Take care, my dear, and keep me abreast of your efforts."

Chapter Twenty-Two

When Beckett entered the room, he smirked. The unattractive smile marred his already damaged face. "Was that my lovely wife who just left?"

"You needn't worry; she came to inform us that she is seeking a divorce, so soon she won't be your concern."

The shocked expression on Beckett's face morphed into amusement.

"The justices won't agree to a divorce unless she has strong male support. Who knows enough about our marriage to support her in her foolish endeavour?"

Sir George scowled at his son. "I'm glad you find Layla's distress so amusing. Her Father knows what has transpired throughout your marriage. Have you forgotten that he sent her the horse and a stable boy? When the thugs you hired beat the boy and attempted to kill Layla and Tilly, Lord Buckingham sent Jack for her protection and a carriage and horses, so she wasn't confined to the estate. At the same time, you accompanied your mistress to events your wife should have attended, and the Buckingham estate is not so isolated that your shenanigans were not reported."

Beckett had lost the cocky attitude before he said, "Surely Lord Buckingham won't pursue the divorce application; it would ruin Layla."

"Her marriage to you was supposed to save her reputation, which didn't work because you made certain it didn't work. Layla said she would rather the divorce ruin her than live here as your abandoned wife. And son, make no mistake, if Layla needs extra support, I will provide it."

Beckett looked appalled. "You would support my wife and not me?"

"Why do you need support? Everything Layla is accusing you of is factual. I'm unsure why you imagined she would wait years for you to come around, but your time is up. You can hide and become a hermit unless you make some serious restitution. Have you looked in the mirror lately? You look like a homeless man. You told your Mother and me that your friend died after saving you, yet you tarnish his sacrifice by refusing to live outside this house. Would he have made that sacrifice if he had known that you would return to England and hide away for the rest of your life? If this behaviour is the best you can manage, your friend made a bad bargain."

"Look at my face! Ahmed would have understood my reluctance to subject myself to ridicule. I can't subject anyone, apart from you and Mother, to seeing this face. I've done Layla a favour by refusing to see her; I don't need my wife swooning at the sight of my monstrous face."

Sir George shook his head. "In the time you spent with Layla, which I concede was limited, did you see her swoon regularly? The first time she called for help with the grooms, I nearly swooned from the stench, but Layla placed a kerchief against her nose and carried on. She spends time with the men from the rehabilitation centre, some of whom have life-changing injuries. Your wife is a feisty, brave woman with more compassion than anyone I've ever met. Did you allow her to make her own decision about whether to see you or not? Are you doing your son a favour by never meeting him? Man up, Beckett, and if you want your wife, if you want a life, I suggest you start with a haircut, a shave and a bath."

Sir George left the room, and Beckett slumped in an armchair. Had he handled this situation all wrong, as his Father suggested? If Beckett had considered the facts and not jumped to conclusions, he would have realised that Layla visited severely injured men weekly without a qualm. He hadn't allowed her to see the damage on his face and had pushed her away with lies and tales of fictitious mistresses. Beckett reviewed his Father's words. Did Ahmed make a fruitless sacrifice if he remained home, nursing his fears and insecurities?

When Beckett left the room, he walked to where the butler stood, face averted as he had demanded.

"Grimes, you may look at me. I am no longer hiding. Could you direct the footmen to prepare a bath in my room and ask my Father's valet to attend me?"

"Yes, sir Beckett."

As Beckett climbed the stairs to his bedroom, he shook his head. When directed to look at him, Grimes had not flinched or given any indication that Beckett's face was anything but ordinary. Could he go out in public without shrieks of horror and disgust? Once the valet helped clean him up, Beckett would put his question to the test.

When Beckett entered the dining room, his Mother's surprised exclamation stopped him in his tracks. Lady Fitzwilliam's eyes welled with tears as she hurried around the table to stand before Beckett.

"Oh, my goodness, you look so handsome with your haircut and the beard trimmed."

She smiled as she said, "The eye patch is very dashing. What brought on this change?"

Sir George, who had entered the room while his wife scrutinised Beckett's appearance, smiled and said, "Good choice, son."

Lady Fitzwilliam retook her chair and said, "I assume you have something to do with this transformation, George."

George smiled but allowed Beckett to explain. Once Beckett recounted the conversation between his father and himself, Lady Fitzwilliam said, "So you are going to try to convince Layla not to proceed with the divorce?"

"I have committed so many sins against her that I doubt that I can convince her to give me another chance. I have a son I have never seen, and during her confinement, while I was absent, Tilly and Jack cared for her. When you consider the course of our marriage, it was an unmitigated disaster, and unfortunately, I am almost solely responsible for that."

"When do you intend to visit her? If you don't move quickly, her Father will have her letter asking for his assistance. If the justices move swiftly on the request, you may be divorced before you know it."

"I know. I will send a message asking to see Layla tomorrow, and hopefully, she hasn't sent off her letter already."

Chapter Twenty-Three

Layla looked at the message that Ellis handed to her. After months of wishing to hear from him, Beckett, threatened with divorce, had requested a meeting. Layla wondered if she should subject herself to her husband's bad temper and hurtful insults. What could be gained by sitting in the same room and apportioning blame for their failed marriage? Layla hadn't contacted her Father, although, after two or three attempts, she thought she had explained the issue and made the request. Did she wait to send the message after seeing Beckett or follow through on her decision?

The decision to meet with Beckett was a foregone conclusion, and eventually, she decided to send the message to her Father after she had listened to what Beckett had to say. Layla wondered why, after all this time, Beckett had decided to show his face. His reluctance to be seen by people other than his parents was the reason for their latest rift, and she wondered what had caused the change. Layla called her butler to warn him of the upcoming meeting and the chance that they might all be shocked at the damage to Beckett's face, but they must not react.

The following day, when the bell rang, Layla had worked herself into a state of anxiety and considered asking Ellis for a decanter rather than the tea tray. She asked Mrs Hogkin to hold off with refreshments until she sensed Beckett's state of mind; she wasn't serving refreshments to a man who couldn't control his temper. When Ellis announced Beckett, Layla rose to greet her husband. His appearance surprised her. On her only visit, Beckett's hair had hung down in greasy clumps, there was the suggestion of a beard, and his clothes were crumpled and odorous. But the man in front of her had neatly trimmed hair and beard and an eyepatch, much to Layla's surprise. His clothes were clean and neatly pressed, and Layla wondered what had prompted the change. Beckett crossed the room, bowed slightly, and asked Layla to sit. She watched as Beckett clenched his fists, and after inhaling, he said, "I guess you are wondering why I am here."

"Yes, that thought crossed my mind, but I am sure you are about to tell me."

"I have much to explain, so if you want to disagree with me, could you wait until the end? I have rehearsed what to say, and I fear I may miss something if I have to answer questions."

Layla nodded her agreement, and Beckett began.

"When I returned from imprisonment, I saw what my parents had told me was true. You were a charming woman, compassionate, kind and spirited. The time we spent together was some of the happiest of my life, and when I left to solve the problems in India, I did intend to return to you. While there, I didn't have a mistress because I discovered before I left that I love you and didn't want another woman, only you. My hateful comments were to push you away because even though I returned, I was not the man you loved. My face is hideous, and I have scars on my back and legs. I feared your rejection, so I rebuffed you first. Can you ever forgive me?"

"What brought on this sudden revelation?"

"There was an uprising while I was in India. The workers wanted a more significant cut of the profits, and if they had come to the office and presented their case, I would have agreed. But in that type of dispute, some rabble-rousers rile the other workers up, and before you know it, the whole thing is out of control. When the situation turned violent, my second-in-command and good friend, Ahmed and I tried to flee. Ahmed was in front of me, and it took him a minute to realise I wasn't behind him. He shot the man with the whip, and the others dispersed. I couldn't walk, so he hid me and fled in search of the troopers. Before they restored order, the mob caught him and hanged him."

As Layla watched the distress on her husband's face, she felt sympathy for the man who lived at the cost of his friend's life. What a heavy burden he carried.

"I am sorry that you have that guilt, but the man obviously thought highly of you, and instead of hiding, you would be better off leaving a lasting legacy for your friend."

"That's close to what my Father said. I was not honouring Ahmed's sacrifice by hiding in my room and pushing you away. My Father suggested I repair the damage I had done in our relationship and then look for ways to celebrate Ahmed's life. He gave his life to save me, and I have to do something to honour him."

"Where does that leave us?"

"The thing I feared about was facing you, yet you haven't recoiled, swooned, or turned away in disgust. Where it leaves us is wherever you are willing to go. I don't want a divorce, and I want to move here to live as we did before I went away and pretend the troubles in between didn't happen, but I know that is too much to ask. I will take whatever part of your life you are willing to share."

"Beckett, you are a fool. The scars change your face, but the important part is what's inside. A kind, loving person with a scarred face is head and shoulders above a handsome face with an ugly personality. You spent so much time feeling wronged and either ignoring my existence or lashing out that you couldn't feel at peace. That period, you say, was the happiest time because we lived in harmony, and if we were to try again, that would be what we would have to do. We did it once, but there is so much water under the bridge that I don't know if we can manage that harmony again."

"Please, Layla, give us a chance."

"The first thing you need to do is meet your son. That is not negotiable, and any chance at being together is null and void if you opt out of meeting him."

"I realise I must meet my son, but what if I scare him?"

"He is too tiny to have preconceived ideas about what is normal and what is not. He will get to know you with your scarred face and eventually might ask what caused it, but he will always accept you as his Father."

117

Epilogue

Twelve months later

The number of carriages parked alongside the building pleased Layla. Today was the culmination of months of work, fundraising and building this new home for the orphaned children. Never again should the workers decide whether to feed or clothe the children. Many of the older children had become employed by local businesses, alleviating the strain. While Layla understood the need for servants, she wanted the children to have more choices than to become indentured to a master who gave little thought to his staff.

Much of the funds for the building came from the disposal of the Fitzwilliam's estate in India, which relieved Layla immensely. Once the English parliament passed a law allowing Indian nationals to own businesses in their native country, the riots and discontent ceased, as workers could see a future in cultivating crops.

Today was the official opening of the Ahmed Singh orphanage, and Layla was proud of her husband's achievements. Politicians, dignitaries and the social echelon of the area crowded around, waiting for the official opening so they could view the inside of the building for themselves. Layla hoped the interest would generate more donations, but she knew many attendees didn't care about the orphanage; they wanted the prestige of saying they were present for the opening. When she and Beckett reconciled many months ago, he vowed to leave a legacy for Ahmed, and his success thrilled her. What came next, she was unsure, but whatever her husband decided to tackle, she would support him.

Layla listened to her husband's speech, paying tribute to his friend Ahmed. Layla was proud when Beckett thanked his parents and wife for their suggestions and support. With the ribbon-cutting ceremony over, the visitors streamed into the building to marvel at the new, more workable rooms and spaces for children.

Beckett escorted the dignitaries to the door, but then turned and walked towards his wife. His smile attested to his happiness and pride in completing the complex task of erecting a new orphanage. Before Beckett reached her, two little girls raced towards him.

"Papa, can we see inside?"

Beckett grabbed the girls, tucked them under his arm like parcels, and continued towards his wife. Penny and Sadie shrieked with laughter as Beckett stood them on their feet.

Against the ton's orders not to show emotion, Beckett kissed his wife on the cheek.

"Goodness, wife, I am inundated with daughters. The next offspring must be boys to even up the numbers, or you will outnumber Matty and me."

Layla laughed. "Let's leave the discussion about more offspring for later and show the girls inside the building."

Layla watched the two little girls hanging onto Beckett's hand as he maneuvered them through the crowd. Layla was aware that some frowned on her for adopting the girls, but after her troubled past with society, she did not care what people thought. Her parents and in-laws had accepted Penny and Sadie as their granddaughters, which was all that mattered. Layla knew there might be rocky times ahead as the girls grew, but her love for them outweighed any troubles.

As they reached the building, Layla squeezed Beckett's arm.

"I am so proud of you."

"Sweetheart, I have never been happier. With you, Matty and the girls, I can conquer any trouble. Thank you for your forgiveness and loving heart. I never thought I wanted many kids, but we look like having enough for a football team.".

Layla laughed. "Not if I have to birth them; we won't."

Also by Robyn C Rye

Farnsworth Sisters
Marrying a Rogue
Rescuing Hannah

The Buckingham Sisters
Lady Maggie's Challenge
Layla's Unwanted Husband

The Evans Family
Sometimes Love is not Enough
Still the One
Moving Forward

Standalone
One More Chance
Lady Jayne's Reputation
Third Time's the Charm
Can't Stop Loving You

The Marriage Scam
An Unlikely Match
Searching For You
The Unexpected Suitor
The Lady and the Duke
Starting Over
An Unforgettable Stranger
The Duke's Revenge
The Temporary Wife
Against The Odds
Betrayed
No Good Turn Goes Unpunished
Lady Eloise's Soldier
Lillian's Forbidden Beau
Remember Me
Always Second Best
When One Door Closes
Coming Home to You
Chasing Shadows
Fool Me Once
Deserting Lady Audrey
My Unlikely Saviour
Lies and Deception
A New Beginning
Julia's Second Chance
The Hidden Enemy
The Maiden's Redemption
Miss Elizabeth's Season